D0651800

The Housewife Assassin's

Relationship Survival Guide

A Novel By

Josie Brown

Published by Signal Press Books

San Francisco, CA

mail@SignalEditorial.com

Book published by Signal Press / San Francisco, CA

Library of Congress Cataloging-in-Publication Data is available upon request

Cover Design by Andrew Brown, ClickTwiceDesign.com

Hardcover ISBN: 978-1-942052-27-2

Trade Paperback ISBN: 978-1-942052-13-5

Praise for Josie Brown's Novels

"This is a super sexy and fun read that you shouldn't miss! A kick ass woman that can literally kick ass as well as cook and clean. Donna gives a whole new meaning to "taking out the trash."

—Mary Jacobs, *Book Hounds Reviews*

"*The Housewife Assassin's Handbook* by Josie Brown is a fun, sexy and intriguing mystery. Donna Stone is a great heroine—housewives can lead all sorts of double lives, but as an assassin? Who would have seen that one coming? It's a fast-paced read, the gadgets are awesome, and I could just picture Donna fighting off Russian gangsters and skinheads all the while having a pie at home cooling on the windowsill. As a housewife myself, this book was a fantastic escape that had me dreaming "if only" the whole way through. The book doesn't take itself too seriously, which makes for the perfect combination of mystery and humour."

—Curled Up with a Good Book and a Cup of Tea

"*The Housewife Assassin's Handbook* is a hilarious, laugh-out-loud read. Donna is a fantastic character–practical, witty, and kick-ass tough. There's plenty of action–both in and out of the bedroom... I especially love the housekeeping tips at the start of each chapter–each with its own deadly twist! This book is perfect for relaxing in the bath with after a long day. I can't wait to read the next in the series. Highly Recommended!"

—CrimeThrillerGirl.com

"This was an addictive read–gritty but funny at the same time. I ended up reading it in just one evening and couldn't go to sleep until I knew what the outcome would be! It was action-packed and humorous from the start, and that continued throughout, I was pleased to discover that this is the first of a series and look forward to getting my hands on Book Two so I can see where life takes Donna and her family next!"

—Me, My Books, and I

"The two halves of Donna's life make sense. As you follow her story, there's no point where you think of her as "Assassin Donna" vs. "Mummy Donna', her attitude to life is even throughout. I really like how well this is done. And as for Jack. I'll have one of those, please?"

—The Northern Witch's Book Blog

Novels in The Housewife Assassin Series

The Housewife Assassin's Handbook
(Book 1)

The Housewife Assassin's Guide to Gracious Killing
(Book 2)

The Housewife Assassin's Killer Christmas Tips
(Book 3)

The Housewife Assassin's Relationship Survival Guide
(Book 4)

The Housewife Assassin's Vacation to Die For
(Book 5)

The Housewife Assassin's Recipes for Disaster
(Book 6)

The Housewife Assassin's Hollywood Scream Play
(Book 7)

The Housewife Assassin's Deadly Dossier
(The Series Prequel)

The Housewife Assassin's Killer App
(Book 8)

The Housewife Assassin's Hostage Hosting Tips
(Book 9)

The Housewife Assassin's Garden of Deadly Delights
(Book 10)

The Housewife Assassin's Tips for Weddings, Weapons, and Warfare
(Book 11)

Chapter 1

Dumping Mr. Wrong

Before you find Mr. Right, you must disentangle yourself from any relationship holding you back.

This is not always easy to do. Despite his lies and cheating, he's grown accustomed to your face.

Not to mention your place, your cooking, and that thing you do with your tongue, which proves you can tie a knot in a cherry stem, no problem.

So, what hints should you give him that it's time to move on?

Start by tossing his stuff out the door.

If he's clueless after that, change the locks and get a restraining order.

If by some off chance he still doesn't get it, invite him into your bedroom. But don't do that thing with your tongue. Instead, just bite down.

Hard.

After he ices down, he'll take the hint and leave. Slowly and hobbling, but certainly it's "Adios."

The best part? Once Mr. Wrong is out the door, the search for Mr. Right can begin!

The digital video being played on the monitor is black and white and grainy, but there is no mistaking the identity of the man being waterboarded:

He is my soon-to-be-ex husband, Carl Alex Stone.

Although it's been two months since I last saw him, even the filthy netting over his head can't hide the profile I know so well. Granted, his frame is thinner than it's ever been, but there is still a weightlifter's definition to his broad shoulders, muscular biceps and rock hard abs, which involuntarily strain each time a steady stream of water, poured from a bucket held by his torturer, drenches the towel periodically thrown over his face.

Despite all the gagging and choking, he won't give them what they ask for: the names of the eleven men who lead the Quorum, a well-funded international terrorist organization.

Instead, he passes out. Five times, in fact.

He always was a stubborn son of a bitch.

I'm watching this video inside a glass-paneled observers' gallery within the United States Naval Station at Guantanamo Bay, where Carl's military commission trial for terror and treason is taking place.

Carl sits only fifty feet from me. While here, he is only acknowledged as Prisoner 1982. But for his trial he is allowed to forgo his usual garb—orange jumper—for a suit, which hangs loosely on him. I'm sure that, when he had it custom made, it fit his body like a glove.

Yes, he knows I'm here. When he shuffled into the room, his legs chained together, he threw me a kiss.

I have the good sense not to shoot him a bird.

Instead, I ignore him. In all honesty, I should be rejoicing. Since the day I learned he was still alive and what he'd become, I dreamt of waterboarding him myself.

So, why don't I feel redeemed?

Over the protests of the prosecuting officer, Army Major Blake Reynolds, the footage of Carl's torture was provided by his lead defense attorney, Mason Lynch. "As you can see, your honor, despite these egregious breaches of the Geneva Conventions, the prisoner's will was never broken. That alone should prove his innocence."

Lynch's declaration is tinged with just enough righteous indignation to elicit an involuntary wince from the judge, Army Colonel Lawrence Cromwell.

"He has steadfastly declared his innocence," Lynch continues.

"Carl Stone is just an American citizen who happened to be at the wrong place at the wrong time. One who, in the past, has served his country admirably, I might add."

Judge Cromwell looks down at the pad in front of him. A prisoner's claim of torture is one thing. Having been presented with physical evidence of torture while in captivity puts this judge in a difficult position. In any other courtroom, this case would have been thrown out before coming to trial. But considering Gitmo prisoners don't exactly get the same due diligence as the rest of us on the US mainland, this is no ordinary trial, and Carl is no ordinary prisoner. Like all of Gitmo's detainees, he is classified as an "unlawful combatant." In fact, at the time of his capture, he was Number 4 on the International Terrorist Watch List.

Not exactly great husband material, don't you agree?

Major Reynolds frowns. He's not just being outmaneuvered, but outclassed, too. You see, unlike the typical legal eagles who defend Gitmo prisoners, Mason Lynch isn't just some civil liberties watchdog or court-appointed JAG officer. He's a litigator who hails from a firm with a quadruple-A Martindale-Hubbell rating.

In other words, he's the best lawyer money can buy.

Not Carl's money, but the Quorum's. He is the organization's best hard man, its most precious asset. The Quorum is wise to protect him at all costs.

Besides, he knows where all the bodies are buried.

More importantly, he knows the identities and locations of the eleven Quorum leaders who are still alive.

Truth be known, Carl has already buried two of them. The first was the military industrialist Jonah Breck, whose computer holds the names of others. My black-ops employer, Acme Industries, has been trying to break the encryption since it fell into our hands.

If Carl had broken under torture, we'd have put them all in jail by now. Something tells me playing good cop wouldn't have gotten us what we wanted, either. At the same time, we can't let their names go to the grave with him. That's where I come in.

Soon, very soon.

Carl left me six years ago, on the night I went into labor with our youngest daughter. I thought he had died in the blaze of a car crash, at the hands of the Quorum. Becoming an assassin for the good guys was my way of avenging his death by destroying the Quorum.

Now this goal includes Carl.

It's why I'm here today. Until our divorce is final, a wife can't testify against her husband.

But I can watch as he is sentenced to pay his debt to society.

Besides, I want to make sure joint custody isn't in the picture.

When it comes to the divorce, Carl has made my life miserable. When he was on the outside, he was great at dodging my subpoenas. Now that he sees the writing on the wall, he insists on joint custody and weekends with our children.

Considering that Gitmo doesn't allow family sleepovers, it's a non-starter. I mean, come on already. It ain't exactly a Disney vacation.

Besides, my children don't know him from Adam. Or more honestly, they don't know him from Jack. More specifically, Jack Craig, who assumed Carl's identity of workaholic-slash- road warrior-slash- loving father. Before Jack's arrival, they presumed their father was on the longest road trip in history: over five years.

Shame on Carl for deserting them. For deserting *me*.

So yeah, he'll get back in their lives *over my dead body*.

Or his, if both the U.S. Government and I get our way.

Jack is also the new man in my life. If Carl had his way, Jack would be dead. He was, for a while. He faked his death, which allowed us to capture Carl.

Losing Jack was a wake-up call for me. If, by some strange twist of fate, Carl walks away from this, I'll kill him myself.

Or die trying.

But first things first: take down the Quorum. For that, we still need Carl.

"Your honor, I'd like to call a few witnesses who can outline fully the scope of Mr. Stone's treason."

The judge nods.

"Jack Craig, will you please take the stand," Blake Reynolds says.

Jack does as he's told. As always, his gaze is intense, but for once his face is as expressionless as a block of concrete. His voice is devoid of passion as he lists Carl's many misdeeds: mostly hits, but thankfully some misses, including two of which I was personally involved in. The first was a plot involving a toxic nanobomb, which we stopped from detonating during the World Little League Series. Jack and I took Carl down during his latest terror attempt, in which he tried to shoot down POTUS in Air Force One with a heat-seeking missile, while it was on final approach into LAX.

You can see why I think Carl is a lousy role model for our kids.

When Jack is done with his testimony, Judge Crowley's face is certainly easy to read: Carl is not long for this world.

Mason Lynch's cross examination doesn't take long. How can you poke holes in evidence that is backed up by photos and video taken at the scenes of Carl's crimes, and with affidavits of several of LA's finest? Not to mention a variety of physical evidence, such as the missile launcher and the now diffused nanobomb.

Ah, boys and their toys.

All eyes turn to Carl. His Mona Lisa smile does not betray the seething anger I know is roiling within him. He has always hated Jack. Before, it was because of his relationship with me. But now he's got a different excuse. Jack has just put the noose around his neck.

When Jack's testimony is finished, he joins me in the observers' gallery. He squeezes my hand as he sits down beside me. I squeeze back. Like him, I'm relieved this chapter in our lives is almost over.

But no, it isn't.

If I'd presumed Jack was the star witness, I'm wrong. "Will Valentina Petrescu please take the stand," Reynolds calls out.

What... the hell?

Valentina is a double agent. Or triple, depending on who you believe: that is, me, or Jack.

Jack avoids my stare. I can easily guess why. Three months ago, Valentina went off the grid, whereabouts unknown. That was fine with me. Her appearance in our lives had me doubting Jack's love.

Quite frankly, seeing her here doesn't help our trust issues.

In our business, pulling an all-nighter is business as usual. In the past few months, Jack has had more than his fair share. I never ask him what he does, since Acme protocol is strict: operatives are only informed on a need-to-know basis.

So, now I know his latest mission involved prepping the testimony of the same comely ex-Romanian gymnast who once broke his heart.

You see, she's also Jack's estranged wife.

Oh yeah, and she ran away with my soon to be ex-husband. He taught her the skills needed to become one of the Quorum's deadliest killers.

But this isn't a lonely hearts club, so Jack and I have had to suck it up and move on. Revenge is a dish best served in jail.

I slip my hand out from under his. Because he doesn't reach for it again, I know he gets it: I'm angry. And yes, I'm hurt.

And no, it will be a long time before I forgive and forget.

One thing that won't fade from memory anytime soon is her attempt to kill me.

She better not catch herself alone with me. I live to return the favor. Despite Jack's conviction that she was just a pawn in Carl's unholy game of world domination, I know better.

She was playing for keeps. And what she wanted didn't include Jack.

She told me so herself.

She is dressed primly, in a high-necked tailored linen suit that defies Cuba's sultry heat. The only indication she is feeling any discomfort at all are the few damp tendrils which have escaped from her otherwise smooth ash blond chignon. Her voice, though low, never wavers. Her tale not only corroborates what we know to be true, it's done with such conviction that even Lynch can't shake her under cross-examination, but he's sure as hell trying.

"Why should anyone believe you, when what you say is the only thing that keeps you from being locked in this hellhole alongside Carl Stone, facing a death sentence?" Lynch snarls at her.

"Because I—" she hesitates a moment, then: "Because I was deceived by him, too."

"You're lying," Lynch declares. "You're here because you're a woman scorned."

"No!" Her Romanian accent is more prominent, now that she's upset. "I'm a woman afraid of a monster who hates everyone, and everything. What he loves is power. I know firsthand the pain he can cause, and the harm he will do, if he's allowed to walk free. "

Unfortunately for Valentina, the only person who hates her more than me is Carl. Her testimony here assures this.

When she steps off the witness stand, she has to pass right by him. Her eyes are drawn to Carl's. His glare makes her flinch in fear. All the color leaves her face. She steadies herself as she stumbles past him, to one of the courtroom's rear benches.

Judge Crowley's deliberation is short. No one is surprised when he delivers a verdict of treason and a sentence of death by lethal injection.

Jack breathes a slight sigh.

I turn my head so that he can't see my response. I wish I could control the tears that rim my eyes.

He must know how I feel anyway, because he asks, "Are you sure you're up for a final farewell?"

During pre-trial negotiations, Lynch was able to wangle a solid concession: a final meeting between Carl and me.

"It works to Acme's advantage. So be it." I shrug. "Besides, I need closure. It will be my last face-to-face with Carl. There's some solace in that."

As I grab my purse and head for the door, he murmurs, "Don't do anything I wouldn't."

That's just it. I know he'd do anything and everything to take down the Quorum.

And he knows I will, too.

It's been a while since Carl has been with a woman. I don't know what he has in mind for me. No matter. It'll be worth it, if he gives up the Quorum.

If he doesn't do so willingly, there's always Plan B.

My first stop is the lady's room. If I'm going to give my ex a final kiss goodbye, I'll need a new coat of lipstick.

In other words, Plan B.

Acme has some special lipstick wands for honeypots like me. For example, the one labeled "Cherry Noir" puts my paramours to sleep. Another, "Murder by Mauve," contains a deadly poison. Since the goal is to get Carl talking, "Chatty Cranberry," which contains the truth drug SP-117, should do the trick.

I've just applied the protective undercoat of gloss that keeps me from reacting to Chatty Cranberry's active ingredient when I hear a retching sound coming from one of the toilet stalls. While faking deep concentration on my beauty regime, through the mirror I keep my eye on the stall.

A moment later the stall door opens and Valentina comes out, dabbing her mouth with a tissue. Now that her jacket is off, the toll the trial has been taking on her is more visible. There are damp spots under the armpits of her blouse. The buttons strain against her very full breasts.

Slowly, I reach for the *Murder by Mauve*. In no time at all, it's open. I palm it like a stiletto, in my left hand. All it takes is a quick slash across her lips, and she's a goner—

And whoever finds her will click their tongues over the heart attack that took one so young and so beautiful.

Boo hoo hoo. It was the false intel she gave me that almost put Jack in his grave. Let's just call this tit for tat.

Apparently Valentina hadn't realized someone else was here. When she sees it's me, her red-rimmed eyes grow enormous. Without thinking, her hand goes to her belly.

She has...

A baby bump.

It's barely there. Only another mother would notice, and not even by the curve.

It's her protective stance that gives her away.

Her eyes follow mine, down to her waistline, but only for a moment. When our eyes meet again, it's in the mirror.

It's hard to apply Chatty Cranberry with a shaky hand.

It's even harder to toss the *Murder by Mauve* wand back in my handbag. Carrying a terrorist's child is a life sentence for any woman. I know this firsthand.

Besides, my goal is not to put her out of her misery, but to prolong it.

When I know I can speak without a quiver in my voice, I murmur, "You're, what, six weeks along?"

She nods.

"So that's why you took off."

"He has children. *Your children.*" Each syllable is weighted with wistfulness, every word blatantly envious. "He would not have wanted the child, and I would never have given it up. I made the necessary choice."

Frankly, I think she's wrong. Carl would want to know, if only to use the kid as a chip in the emotional poker game he plays with her.

The same way in which he uses the threat of taking our children from me.

By dropping my hands to my side, I signal her that she's free to leave; that as far as I'm concerned, there's no longer a target on her head.

There will be no long kiss goodbye. For now, anyway.

She acknowledges my gift with a slight bow.

She heads for the door, but stops when she reaches the threshold, and turns around. "He doesn't know about this, if you're wondering."

This is her way of asking me to keep her secret.

Knowing how Carl likes to shoot the messenger—really, to shoot anyone who gets in his way—I've got no problem sparing him this bit of news.

The door squeaks as it shuts behind her.

I have to redo my lip gloss. I look like a clown, and this is no laughing matter.

My children will soon have a half-sibling. I'll be tied to Valentina for the rest of our lives.

And so will Jack.

I wonder if she told him about the pregnancy.

If it turns out he doesn't know about it, he's not hearing it from me. As it is, his feelings about her are too raw for that little bombshell. The last thing I need is for him to feel sorry for her.

"I'm glad you came. This last time anyway." Carl smiles at his own double entendre.

His attempt at gallows humor leaves a lot to be desired.

The prisoner's visitor gallery inside Gitmo's classified facility known as Camp 7 is nothing fancy. It was constructed from cinder block. Its sole window is barred, and wrapped in steel mesh, allowing the moist Caribbean air to waft through. The two armed guards posted outside the door are part of the Marine Corps' Task Force Platinum. But even that battalion is just the first layer of the security onion in which Carl and other high value detainees are cloistered.

The guards kept their eyes straight ahead, but their lips curled into a smirk when I entered the room.

That's okay. Whatever strings Carl and his lawyers pulled to get me up close and personal with him works to Acme's favor, if I can get him to spill his guts on the Quorum.

"We both want closure, Carl. That is why I'm here." As I sit down across from him, I place my hands on the table between us. "Time to cut a deal, don't you think? Now that the Quorum sees you as a lost cause, it won't care if the government puts a needle into your arm."

I tilt my head toward Mason Lynch, who sits in a chair off to one side. He's engrossed in some legal brief. I wonder if it has anything at all to do with Carl's case, or if he's already moved on from what is obviously a lost cause. As soon as this little tête-a-tête is over, his private Gulfstream G650, sitting on Gitmo's runway, is ready to whisk him back to his gilded Manhattan cage on Lexington Avenue.

When I came in, Lynch rose and shook my hand to thank me for coming. I grabbed his arm with both hands, which gave me a perfect opportunity to slip a sticky GPS microdot inside the pocket of his jacket. My hope is that his first stop will be the offices of his client, the Quorum, to deliver the bad news of Carl's sentence.

Carl's response to my remark is a snort. "I guess you're right. Either way, I'm a dead man. Maybe it will be a shiv in the shower. Or maybe I'm in for another rambunctious round of waterboarding."

"I can help you, Carl. Just give us the names, and before I leave Guantanamo, you'll have a deal that will allow you to leave with me, and to live your life incognito."

"Don't be such a silly little fool, Donna."

"I'm trying to save you! Do you think the Quorum could find

you, even with your knowledge of spycraft and a deal that includes Witness Protection?"

"But of course! It's a sea serpent with 11 heads and tentacles in every nook and cranny of our government, including the Department of Justice." Even facing the gallows, he can crack a smile. "But I invite you to ply your coquettish wiles in an effort to change my mind."

Finally, his hand reaches for mine.

When I don't pull away, his eyes seek mine out. "I can't bear the thought of never seeing you again," he mutters.

There's a part of me that would still like to believe he has feelings for anything; not necessarily me, but perhaps for the life we once shared. Or at least for our children. This thought makes it easy for me to tear up. "Carl, why did you ask for me?"

"Didn't they tell you? My death row wish is a conjugal visit."

Seeing my glower, he laughs and adds, "Oh, quit playing hard to get. You know you want it, too." His smirk fades. "Truth is I have something for you. I can't make up for all the sorrow I've caused you, but I hope it redeems me in your eyes somewhat."

He snaps his fingers at Lynch, who looks up, startled. "That little item I asked you to get from my safety deposit box: did you bring it?"

"I have it right here." Lynch picks up his valise and walks over to us. When he opens it, he pulls out a box and puts it between Carl and me.

"Go on, open it," Carl says.

"I take off the rubber band, and then open the lid. Inside are photos from his childhood, which had disappeared with him. Also in the box are an old Bible and an antique brooch.

I recognize both items. They belonged to Carl's grandmother. "I... you want me to have these?"

"Sure, why not? They won't do me any good where I'm going. And... well, if you ever tell our children the truth about me, I don't want them to think I was all bad."

"Wow, Carl. I'm touched." I purse my lips, to keep from biting off the Chatty Cranberry.

He takes that as a come-hither look and raises a brow, in anticipation.

Works for me. Anything to get him kissing and telling. But I can't seem too anxious, or he'll be suspicious. "I guess one kiss wouldn't hurt. For old time's sake, I mean."

"Yeah, I thought this sentimental tripe would put you in the mood."

Ignoring him, I lean in for the smooch that will have him bearing his soul to me.

Carl has my arm twisted around my back. "Say even one word and I'll break it," he hisses into my ear.

The next thing I know, Carl has pricked my bicep with his Grandmother's broach.

What the hell, I try to say, but the words seem stuck in my mouth. In fact my whole body seems to be freezing up.

I've been drugged.

In no time, Lynch is on his feet. He glances at the guards. His lawyerly instincts are to protect his client. Seeing that the Marines still have their backs to us, he rushes over and hisses, "Carl, please don't do anything that will make things worse."

Carl's elbow hits Lynch's gut. The lawyer doubles over, but before he can scream, Carl's fist slams into his windpipe. As Lynch blacks out, Carl grabs Lynch's head between his hands and breaks his neck with one quick twist, catching him when he falls.

I watch, frozen and helpless, as Carl eases Lynch into the chair which puts Lynch's back to the door. Then Carl grabs the Bible. When he rips apart the book, a thin latex layer is revealed between its covers: it's a mask of some sort...

Oh my God, it's a replica of Lynch's face.

In no time at all, Carl adheres it onto the top part of his own face, leaving only his mouth and chin free. It's seamless enough that the guards will never notice.

Then he yanks off Lynch's hair.

The guy wears a piece? Go figure...

Taking the mirror out of my purse, Carl adjusts the toupee so that it's a passable fit. Then he strips off his jacket, exchanging it for the dead man's, along with his tie and VIP badge.

Finally, he sets Lynch's hands on the table, clasped together and head bowed, over the Bible.

The color has already drained out of the lawyer's face. His eyes are open wide in fear.

If I could, I'd throw up.

Carl, you're one sick fuck.

I'm next. In no time at all Carl lifts me onto my feet. With his arm around my waist, he propels me forward. Like the rest of me, my legs are numb, but at least they're moving, which is more than I can say for my mouth, which seems to be filled with sand.

"How do you like my little zombie prick? It's my very own concoction: some neuromuscular block to shut your trap, and just enough scopolamine to keep you docile. Makes you the perfect Stepford Wife. Ha! I should have thought of this, years ago! We might still be together."

In your sick dreams.

Right before we go out the door, Carl tilts my head onto his shoulder and pats it gently, as if I'm prostrate with grief.

My face is angled in such a way that I only catch a glimpse of the guards for a second. To my dismay, they give us no more than a cursory nod.

We are just a few steps beyond them when Carl turns back and says, "My client is depressed over the news that his wife here is divorcing him. Since the judge has allotted him a full hour's visitation privilege, I presume you'll honor the time he has left, so that he can pray for his soul in this hour of need."

His polite "Thank you" indicates they've nodded at his request.

He's been granted the time to make his getaway, with me as his hostage.

He pushes me out of the building and over toward Gitmo's landing strip, holding a one-way conversation as if he doesn't have a care in the world.

"Time for a little ride, doll. Should be fun! I've booked an entire island, just for the two of us. Well, for you, really: Musha Cay. Trust me, you'll love it! Dig this: a two-mile long private sand bar, beds galore in all five sumptuous villas. In other words, paradise."

He pauses to wipe the drool off my chin, and to nudge my lips into a smile. In the process, he smears my lipstick, frowns, and wipes it off on the crisp kerchief in what had been the chest pocket of Lynch's jacket.

The initials embroidered on the kerchief, *ML*, are now smeared with Chatty Cranberry. There goes Plan B.

"Hey, did you happen to pack a bikini?" Carl asks. "No? That's okay. You'll have an awesome all-over tan when they come for you. Too bad I can't keep you company, but someone has to take the fall for my little disappearing act. It makes sense that it's you, what with the way you've been pining after me all these years."

When they come for me.

Will I be dead, or alive?

He's lucky I'm too weak to talk back.

Or to break his neck.

All I want to do...is...

Sleep.

I wake to the sounds of waves lapping on a distant shore, the squawk of macaws, and the dull drone of sap-thirsty hummingbirds.

I try to raise my arms, but they feel as if they weigh a ton. I have better luck opening an eyelid, but I can't see anything because I'm laying face down. My head is turned to one side, but apparently Carl put a large floppy sun hat over it, which keeps me from seeing what I hear next:

The whisking blades of a helicopter, getting closer and closer.

Until it lands nearby, on Musha Cay's sugary white sandbar;

The gentle crunch of gravel under the boots of the eight members of the SEAL Team 6 Devgro unit as they make their way up the walkway that winds its way from the beach to Musha Cay's five opulent guest villas;

But then they freeze when they come across me, sunning myself on a cushioned chaise¬

And finally, the rush of air as eight HK-MP7a1's are raised and aimed, within inches of me.

Inevitably I hear the team's commander shout, "Donna Stone! Raise your arms over your head! *Now! Now!*"

Of course I can't.

It takes them just a moment to figure out something is wrong. Why else would I still be lying here, motionless and naked, despite their startling commands, not to mention severe sunburn?

My hat falls off as two of the men lift me up from under my arms. I dare to squint up at them, but their profiles are obliterated in a halo of the bright tropical sun.

As they force-march me into the closest villa, one of the SEALs lets loose with a long, appreciative whistle. “Whooeee, damn! She sure is one red hot naked mama!”

I don’t know what hurts more, my overexposed skin or my bruised ego.

Carl is going to pay for this.

Chapter 2

Finding Mr. Right

Your chances of finding Mr. Right are a lot better if you know exactly who you're looking for. Let's make a wish list, shall we?

First, there should be some physical attraction between you. (This isn't to say that he should call out "Hubba, hubba!" or act like a bonobo in heat at the sight of you.)

Next, he should be a gentleman at all times. (This is especially true when he catches you in the throes of passion with your old boyfriend. A gentleman believes a lady when she explains that she lost her contact in her ex's bed, and he was just helping her find it. Naked, of course, because that's how you lost it in the first place.)

And finally, he must be willing to show you a good time. In Paris. Where you will travel on his private jet, and stay at the

Georges Cinq.

What, you're concerned this wish list is too ambitious? You're wrong! The gal who gets her Mr. Right starts with a clear vision of who he is, and emphatically knows she deserves what she gets.

Yep, she's one lucky lady! And that lady could be you.

Carl was right. Musha Cay's villas are to die for.

Considering my dire situation, maybe I should rephrase that.

Granted, I'm basing this solely on the villa set up as my own personal party central. The décor is plantation shabby chic, with lazy fans, gauzy drapes, wide-plank bleached bamboo floors, and large shutters, folded back to frame a baby blue horizon.

French doors lead to a master suite, where the virginal white cotton sheets covering the Cal king bed are strewn with the accoutrements of illicit pleasures soon to be enjoyed: a rainbow array of thong bikinis, a couple of sheer negligees, a treasure chest of sex toys—

Oh, and let's not forget the ten six-inch bricks of Euro banknotes in €500 denominations, or the Swiss bank account statement showing a week-old deposit of thirty million dollars.

All of which are being dusted for fingerprints right now.

Guess whose they'll find on it?

Major Reynolds and Jack look up as Seal Team Donna tosses

me into a large wingback chair. Their faces are a contrast of emotions. While Reynolds' darkens into a knowing grimace, Jack's softens with relief at seeing me alive before clouding over with worry at my predicament.

Guess which one grabs a terrycloth robe off the bed and drapes it over me?

"Lady, I don't need to tell you things don't look so good for you." Major Reynolds leans into me. "Until Prisoner 1982, no one—I repeat, *no one*—has ever escaped from Gitmo. As his accomplice, I can take you back there, and detain you as a terrorist, not to mention charge you for the murder of an innocent civilian. So start talking. Where is he?"

"How the hell should I know? Lynch's plane has GPS. Why aren't you tracking it?" My words spill out of me at the speed of molasses on a frosty morn. "And for the record, I didn't help Carl escape! I was drugged!"

"That's great, Donna," Jack says hopefully. "A simple blood and urine test proves you right, and we're out of here." He motions to one of the SEALs, who nods and reaches into his gunny sack for the testing apparatus.

I wince. "You won't find anything. Whatever Carl gave me didn't leave traceable evidence."

Reynolds laughs raucously at what he considers to be a tall tale.

A decorative letter opener, left on an antique book bedside table by my chair, has found its way into the sleeve of my robe, go figure.

Jack notices this miracle and shakes his head slightly.

Yeah, okay, I'll keep my cool. For now.

Jack turns back to Reynolds. "Lynch's pilot—or, I guess the Quorum's—diverted from the flight plan's original destination, Teterboro Airport. It shows good faith on Donna's part that she put the GPS microdot on Lynch's jacket. We would not have found her so quickly if she hadn't. Unfortunately for you, Donna, Carl changed his clothes here before heading off to parts unknown. We found the jacket and the rest of Lynch's suit under this bed."

"Mr. Craig has fully informed me about your asset's history," Reynolds butts in. "But it's your relationship with the prisoner that concerns me even more." He weighs a Euro brick in each hand before tossing them back on the bed. "Black-ops freelancers get turned all the time, especially when personal feelings are part of the mix."

I smile. "Let me make this perfectly clear, Major Reynolds. The only emotion I feel for my ex is hate."

"Then enlighten us, Mrs. Stone. Why don't the facts as you present them add up? You're seen walking out with the prisoner. There was no gun held to your head. In fact, you're smiling, as if you don't have a care in the world. Then you take the dead man's private jet to an exclusive private island, off American soil. To top it off, you're found with a bag full of money, and the proof that more funds have been deposited in your name in an offshore bank account. So, why should I believe anything you say?"

I may be fully awake now, but I feel as if I'm still in a very bad dream. "For God's sake, can't you see? I've been set up!"

Reynolds shrugs. He's not buying it.

"Unfortunately, you'll have to prove it from a Gitmo jail cell." The son of a bitch paces in front of me, as if practicing his spiel in front of a jury. "You're the worst kind of traitor, Donna Stone: a bored American housewife who wants the thrill of playing the honeypot whore while the kiddies are in school. I guess when your terrorist hubby offered you a chance to join him and leave your mundane life behind, you just couldn't say no!"

It's my turn to laugh. "If that's your take on women who do what they can to earn a living when left to raise their children on their own, it's no surprise you're not married. Newsflash, Major: This isn't the *Housewives of the CIA*. Admit it. You've been outsmarted by a prisoner more connected than you'll ever be. Now, let us do our work, which is to find him."

Reynolds' face turns as purple as a Thai eggplant, which reminds me: I've still got the grocery shopping to tackle when I get back home.

"I've had enough of your crap—" Reynolds begins, but he's interrupted by the appearance of an armed guard, who murmurs something too low for me to hear.

Reynolds squints in disbelief. "You're sure?"

The guard nods.

"Stay here," Reynolds warns the guard. "Don't let either of these people out of your sight."

Silently, Jack slides down into a chair. I shrug. Seeing this, Reynolds steps outside onto the veranda.

We can hear him bark, “Yes sir, but—” several times until he lets loose with a deflated “Yes, sir!”

He’s still glowering as he storms back into the room. He nods to the sentry. “Unlock the lady.”

The sentry murmurs his own “Yes, sir” and my arm charms are off, finally.

“At least someone believes the baloney you’re serving up, Mrs. Stone.” Reynolds’ dark glare is proof I’m not out of the woods yet. “The CIA director has agreed that house arrest back in Hilldale, California will do—for now. You’re to be monitored with an ankle bracelet until we’re able to validate your story. In the meantime, if we find Prisoner 1982 anywhere near you, or if we find proof that you had anything to do with his escape, you’ll find yourself back at Guantanamo, answering to me. Do you understand?”

I tilt my head to gauge the distance I’d have to throw the letter opener in order to pierce this jerk right between the eyes.

As if reading my mind, Jack answers, “We thoroughly understand, Major.”

Then he yanks me up out of the chair and hustles me out the door, catching the letter opener as it slides out of my sleeve.

Spoil sport.

“Donna, quit squirming! I’m spreading more of this aloe goop on the carpet than on your back.”

"I can't help it! Every time you touch my skin, it burns like hell. And besides, the stuff is ice cold."

"Things could have been worse."

"Oh? How so?" I turn over to face him.

The private plane sent by Ryan Clancy, our boss at Acme Industries, isn't as plush as Lynch's, but it will do. At least the six-hour flight home gives Jack and me one thing: time alone together, without other operatives, let alone our children, and the sideshow acts inherent with raising three kids.

I can think of one very good way we could take advantage of it. Unfortunately, I'm too sore to follow through.

So yeah, I have a right to be grumpy.

Gently but firmly, Jack shoves me back down onto the floor of the plane. His hands are large, but they are also gentle as they massage the lotion into my shoulders. "For starters, Carl could have pushed you out of the plane, and we would have never found your body."

I shrug. "He needed a different kind of fall guy. Or I should say, fall gal."

"I'm sure it's his short-term goal, but he wants you around for the long haul."

"What do you mean by that?" My question comes out in a blissful sigh. Jack's palms circle slowly down my back, kneading muscles still sore from the hours they laid dormant in an outdoor chaise.

"If he kills you, he'll miss the fun of torturing you, one head game at a time." Jack's thumb finds a tight muscle and digs into it. For me, release comes with a groan of pleasure. "Donna, you may not want to admit it to yourself, but he's still in love with you."

I sit up with a yelp. "Bite your tongue!"

"Hey, I call it as I see it." His smile fades. "Not that I can blame him."

I shudder at the thought. "I guess that's one good thing about being under surveillance. Carl can't go anywhere near me unless he wants to risk getting caught." I hesitate, then murmur, "So, when did Valentina contact you?"

His hand, which has been stroking my lower back, pauses for what seems like an eternity. Finally he mutters, "Just last month. She called Acme's secure line, which I'd given her before my 'untimely demise.' With Carl in custody, she felt safe enough to come back into the fold. And she insisted on testifying against him."

"Congratulations for turning her." He can't see my face, but he can read my voice: *Bullshit.*

"You'll never believe that she didn't know the storage unit holding the heat-seeking missile was booby-trapped, will you?"

"No, I won't. I think she knew someone from Acme was going to be blown to smithereens when that door opened. And my guess is she was hoping it was going to be me, not you." I can't help but mutter, "I presume she hightailed it out of Guantanamo the moment she heard Carl flew the coop. She's right to lay low—and as far away as possible."

"Acme promised her safe haven in return for her testimony. We're following through. You know better than anyone Carl has a long memory. After what she said about him, he'll be out for blood." Jack's hands, which have been moving slowly up my spine, stop short. "Is your interest based on your conviction that she still has feelings for me?"

I shrug. I'll never tell him I already know the answer to that. A long time ago, she told me that she envied me: not for Jack's love, but for Carl's obsession.

So no, I don't need to know if she has feelings for him. What I really want to know is if *he* still loves *her*? Does he care about her?

Does he know she's carrying a baby? And if so, does it deepen his feelings for her?

If I come out and ask, will he lie to me?

I find my answer in the way Jack reaches for my waist.

A shiver goes up my spine. I love to feel his hands on me.

And his arms around me.

And his cock inside of me.

The sooner the better, sunburn be damned.

He must feel the same way, because he's lifted me up onto my knees.

Pleasure is his thick thumb and forefinger probing me.

Longing comes with every kiss: on my lips, down my neck, on my nipples, and roaming down, to my pubic mound.

His kisses build my expectation. By the time he enters me, the anticipation is unbearable.

As he pulls me close, I ache with unbound desire and am relieved that I am safely back in his embrace.

Ecstasy is found deep within me, with each of Jack's thrusts. When we orgasm, I arch up into him. Our spasms leave him shuddering inside me.

We lay there for a half hour before he whispers, "I love you, Donna. Always and forever."

"Works for me," I murmur.

What I don't say out loud is that I'll never doubt him again.

We're still sleeping when the plane skids to a stop, back home in Orange County.

Then reality sets in. The fridge is empty. The laundry is sky high. My children need help with their homework.

And Carl is on the loose.

First things first. Lose the ankle bracelet.

That's easier said than done.

CHAPTER 3

SIX VERY BROAD HINTS YOU'RE DATING A SERIAL KILLER

When it comes to our love lives, we presume we have great instincts as to whom we should date. Wrong! Here are six very big hints that the new man in your life may in fact wish to cut it short:

Hint 1: Instead of emails, he sends love letters...but the words are cut out of old magazine headlines.

Hint 2: He insists on being a gentleman and opening the car door...well, in his case, the car's trunk.

Hint 3: Instead of cufflinks at the bottom of his sleeves, he keeps a knife up his sleeve.

Hint 4: After every meal out, he rubs down his fingerprints on all shiny surfaces.

Hint 5: All pictures of his previous "girlfriends" are pinned on the wall of his living room, as part of a montage made up of "Missing Persons."

Hint 6: He likes to entertain you in his basement, where the grand tour includes a coffin which, as he puts it, "I built especially for you. Go ahead, and get in. I want to make sure it fits..."

Big bonus hint: Break up immediately.

Even bigger bonus hint: Run. Fast and far away.

Carl was right. Musha Cay's villas are to die for.

"Donna Stone, I've been ringing your doorbell for the past ten minutes," shouts Penelope Bing, Hilldale's queen bee mean mommy, from my front stoop. "What in hell are you doing up on your roof?"

I peek out from behind my chimney. "Oh! Um...cleaning the gutters, of course!"

It would be too rude to tell her the truth: that I presumed my roof was the only place left to hide from her.

It's been a week since we got home, and still no clearance from the Feds. At the same time, Penelope and her posse—Tiffy Swift, and the unfortunately named Hayley Coxhead—have been relentlessly hunting me down. My guess is that they're trying to recruit me for one of their many harebrained projects.

Just how the heck did she find me?

Ah, I see now: Tiffy is waving to me from her upstairs guest bedroom, beside the high-gauge telescope she has set up in the bay window.

"Well, come on down. Have you forgotten it's your month as Hilldale's Welcome Ambassador?"

Whenever Penelope drops her baton of verbal abuse, her number one lackey, Hayley, eagerly picks it up and beats me over the head with it. "We have three new neighbors! None of them have received their welcome baskets. How are they going to know where to shop without a Hilldale Chamber of Commerce directory?"

I shrug. "Google maps?"

Penelope shakes her head in disgust. "Donna, you may have been raised without any social graces, but we refuse to let it reflect on the rest of us."

Then I guess a SWAT team holding me spread-eagled on the ground and detonating the welcome basket in case it holds an incendiary device won't leave a great impression, either.

But that's the dealio, should I go beyond the perimeter of my yard with this house arrest bracelet on my ankle.

Not that I can say that to Penelope. It would be the scandal of Hilldale.

Penelope sighs mightily. "My God, Donna, get with the program! In fact, we've already done the hard work, putting the gift baskets together. All you have to do is deliver them. Even a trained monkey can do *that*."

From where I sit, I'm within reach of few loose Spanish tile shingles. Should they fall on Penelope, the worst she'd suffer is a concussion.

The thought is tempting enough that I nudge one with my toe—

It stays put, but I go skittering down the roof instead. The only thing that saves me is a drain pipe, just within reach.

I don't know how much longer I can hang on when I hear Jack's car skid into the driveway. At the same time Penelope and Hayley's heads swivel in his direction, Tiffy's telescope zooms in on him, too.

He whistles a happy tune as he hops out. His shirt goes taut over his biceps as he rummages in the car's trunk for his gym bag. Tall, dark, and too handsome for his own good, Jack is catnip to this pride of tiger moms.

He rewards the women with a big smile. "Ah, two of my favorite neighbors! To what do I owe the pleasure?"

Hayley nudges Penelope out of her lust-filled stare. "Unfortunately, Donna has once again dropped the ball on the deliveries of the Hilldale Women's Club Welcome baskets."

"Tsk, tsk! What a naughty girl she's been." Jack's lascivious tone conjures up all sorts of fun and games. Penelope blushes fifty shades of pink.

In her dreams.

He winks at me. "Donna my sweet, do you plan on being up

there much longer?"

"I should be down in a moment." Make that a nanosecond. I'm barely hanging on by my fingertips.

"No rush. Take your time. In fact, I insist on delivering the baskets, as long as Penelope and Hayley tag along to give me directions." As innocent as he sounds, he knows exactly what he's doing.

Both women squeal as they run to the car. Hayley reaches the front passenger door first, but Penelope shoves her aside and jumps in first.

"No! Don't leave yet! Wait for me," Tiffy squeals from the window. She's out her front door so fast that you'd think her house was on fire.

They wave at me as they drive off.

I do the same. Big mistake. I needed both hands to stay aloft.

Thank goodness, I fall into the pool.

My security ankle bracelet is waterproof, so at least a Homeland Security SWAT team won't come running.

I needed to wash my hair, anyway.

"When did you first start having sex?" Mary asks.

Her question causes me to swipe the nail polish brush over her pinky toe, and the one beside it.

It's Day Eight of my lockdown. I was wrong to presume that time would pass quicker if I painted my nails a different color each day. Initially I was able to coerce both Mary and Trisha to join me for my daily pampering session, but yesterday Trisha dropped out, despite the fact that the *colour de jour* was Disney Villain's Cruella De Vil.

Her excuse: "Mommy, Cruella is a meanie. Besides, my toes miss being plain old pink." That was her way of telling me I need a new hobby.

Don't I know it.

Considering the subject at hand, I'm okay that today it's just Mary and me. But let's face it, she's asked a loaded question. Girls have sex so much earlier than we did. (Well, than I did...) If I answer honestly, she may think I was a slut. Or a desperate spinster.

Either way, I come off as a loser.

The GPS security bracelet on my ankle, coupled with freshly painted toes on my left foot, hobble me as I stumble over to the French doors that separate the sunroom from the media room. I lied and told the kids the bracelet was from my doctor, to strengthen my ankle against some imaginary tendonitis.

Now I have a bigger issue to fib about: Sex.

I'm closing the doors so that my ten-year-old son, Jeff, and his pals, Cheever Bing and Morton Smith, can't listen in on our discussion. If anything can tear them away from Minecraft, it's a discussion about S-E-X by two people of the opposite sex, especially if one is Jeff's older sister.

I settle back down onto the couch and try to collect my thoughts before speaking. "I waited until I knew I was with 'the one.'"

I'm lying, of course. Who the hell knows a guy is "the one" when they're seventeen? Or twenty-seven, for that matter.

I guess the proof I guessed wrong was when Carl left me with three kids.

But yes, I presumed he was "the one." What I didn't count on was his also being Public Enemy Number One.

While Mary tries to find meaning in my dodge, I add, "Why exactly do you want to know?"

"Because—" she pauses. "No reason. I was just wondering."

Ah, I see.

Mary is twelve going on twenty, and that freaks me out. Her quote-unquote steady is a cute kid named Trevor Smith, the captain of the Hilldale Middle School varsity basketball team. Right now, I want to break both his arms before he does something to Mary that he'll regret, and she will, too.

"Sex is different from love, Mary."

"Oh, Mom!" Mary rolls her eyes. "I know that!"

"Okay, I'll take your word for it. So, tell me: why are they different?"

She stops to think about it. Then: "When you date, some guys only want to see how far they can get with you. You know...they don't really treat you as a person." She shakes her head sadly. "I don't want to be that kind of girl."

I nod, but say nothing. Inside I'm doing a happy dance because she actually knows the difference.

"But I think it's exciting when a boy—a *guy*—is just as sweet on you as you are on him."

"I can see that." I try to keep my tone nonchalant as I drench a cotton ball in polish remover and wipe off yesterday's sparkly turquoise from Mary's left foot. "But love is different, at different ages and stages of life. And so is dating. That's why it's smart to date more than one guy, so you have some other experiences for comparison. The good guys always show respect, and never push you to—to do anything that doesn't seem right."

"Did you date a lot, before you met Dad?"

"Yes, I'd dated some, but I wasn't that experienced." I'm sure the color of my cheeks is almost as dark and purple as the polish I'm applying to her nails. "I was twenty when we met, and I was in college. We married within a year, after I turned twenty-one."

"Did you feel you should have waited?"

"No. At least, not at the time."

"But in hindsight, would you have liked to have had more experiences?"

"Yes, I wish I had. It's hard to know what's right for you if you've had too few experiences, or have only experienced one relationship that is not really working for you."

Mary looks up sharply. "But Dad wasn't wrong for you, was he?"

Ah, yet another trick question. "Dad has changed a lot over the years. Then again, I have, too. "You see, Mary, not only must you both grow, you can't have grown apart."

"When Dad was gone all that time, did you grow apart?"

Her question rips a tiny tear in my heart. Does she suspect that Jack isn't Carl Stone, her father?

I search her face for the answer. What I see is innocence and curiosity.

And trust.

It's why I can answer her from the bottom of my heart. "To stay in love, you need respect, and passion, and above all, trust. All the time I waited for him, I trusted he would come home again."

Carl never really came home.

On the other hand, Jack has proven to me he is worth the wait.

Mary's comprehension comes with a slow nod. "Mom, I think Trevor likes me as much as I like him, but sometimes I catch him looking at other girls, and that makes me jealous. So I don't know about the 'trust' part. At least, not yet."

"To find true love at such a young age is a rare thing. If it's real, he'll wait until you grow into the woman you were meant to be, and he'll grow up, too. You'll stay friends, but have other friends as well: people who make you laugh, and who you can count on to be there for you, and who will prove their friendship through trust. If he stays your friend, he will be all that, and more."

Mary waits until her toes dry, then she kisses me on the cheek and murmurs, "Don't worry, Mom. I'm not ready for 'that' yet. I'm only asking because I know you'll always tell me the truth."

The truth. Yes, it's what we strive to know.

I pray she never learns the truth about her father.

"Besides," she adds, "when the time comes, you'll be the first to know."

She kisses me on the forehead then runs upstairs to do her homework.

Lucky me.

And no matter where that first boy hides, I will track him down.

"I've got both good news and bad news," Jack declares. "First some good news: I'll be subbing for you in regard to welcome basket drop-off duty. Now, the bad news: your penance is to put the baskets together. But even better news is this: I've arranged for you to skip carpool duty for the next six weeks."

I look up from the couch. I'm so shocked by Jack's declaration that my toenail polishing stops mid-pinky toe on the coffee table. "Oh, my God! You've made a pact with the Devil... I mean, Penelope? I'm almost afraid to ask what you promised her in return. It can't be your 'first born,' since she views Mary as a lost cause. Let me guess: she wants to help you make your fourth."

"My my, you're cute when you're jealous! Okay yeah, invariably all conversations with that woman lead to some intimation that she is ready, willing and able for an exchange of bodily fluids. But you'll be happy to know I let it go right over my head."

I'm tempted to ask: *Which head?* But I think better of it.

I'm afraid of how he'll answer me.

Jack picks up the brush, dips it in the polish then places my foot on his lap. After a few meticulous strokes of *Cruella* on my big toe, I've got one more thing to admire about him.

Talk about the ideal foreplay.

"Unfortunately, I had to give her a realistic excuse as to why you'd be out of commission for so long." He stops to admire his handiwork. "So, listen, when you come in from the cold, don't be surprised if you find Penelope staring at your... chest."

I yank my foot away so fast that he paints a stripe on his khakis. "What the heck did you tell her, anyway?"

"I didn't exactly come out and say anything. It was more like a lightning round of *Twenty Questions*."

The way I'm holding my nail file shows him that, unlike Penelope, I'm not in the mood for any games.

"Okay, if you must know, I inferred you'd be having a few nips and tucks." He points to my breasts.

I stare down at them. "And all this time I thought Pixie and

Dixie were the picture of perfection."

"Baby, you know I do, too! But I had to think fast. Hey, if it makes you feel any better, even she found it hard to believe. When the neighbors call you perky, it ain't your personality they're talking about."

"Gee thanks... I think."

"Don't mention it. In truth, what she bought hook, line and sinker was my hint about a butt lift."

The nail file misses his ear by a mere half inch. He and I both know that if I hadn't been concerned about smearing my manicure, my aim would have been better.

Damn it. Turns out I'm smudged after all. I point this out to him with my middle finger. "You owe me a French Tip."

"Sounds dirty." Tantalized, he arches a brow. "I'm in, but unfortunately it'll have to wait. There's been a break in the case. Ryan's on his way over, with Abu, Arnie and Emma."

"Super. We can have a pajama party."

"Yep, that may be on your agenda, especially if this mission goes down the way I think it will." He frowns. "Arnie has figured out something that all eleven Quorum suspects have in common. Unfortunately, if he's right, only you can infiltrate their club."

"Anything that gets this bracelet off my ankle. Worst. Bling. Ever." I put my leg back in his lap. "Until they get here, make yourself useful. My left foot needs a second coat."

He hesitates, but he knows better than to say no.

The Acme team comes bearing Krispy Kremes.

Not a good sign.

I reach for the doughnuts, but before I can grab a couple of glazed, Jack lifts the box out of reach. "Think 'butt lift'," he mutters out of the corner of his mouth.

Lift *this*.

To stifle the urge to elbow him in the gut, I smile at Ryan. "Welcome! To what do I owe the honor?"

"We've had a breakthrough." He looks over at Jack, who nods and opens the doughnut box for him.

Am I salivating as Ryan pops one into his mouth? You betcha. Some pity party this is turning out to be. "So Jack said, among other things. What's the dealio?"

"As you know, Jonah Breck kept detailed dossiers on each of the twelve other Quorum leaders, but we've yet to break the encryption system used to shield their names and occupations. However, Arnie found one very strange anomaly shared by all of them." Ryan coughs uncomfortably.

"They're all sugar daddies," Arnie blurts out.

I look from one to the other. "Say, what?"

Emma frowns. "As in, older rich dudes who like dating college co-eds for their scintillating conversation. Usually the dates take place in the fancy apartments these douchebags keep for their 'sugar babies,' albeit most of the time their girlfriends are too busy faking orgasms to talk about Proust or Nixonian political strategy."

"Ah. Got it." Suddenly my breasts don't seem so perky. Besides, I never got through *Swann's Way*. Too high falutin'.

"The online service they used to meet these ladies is among Breck Industries' assets. It's called SugarCEOs.com." Ryan pauses. "Breck offered his fellow Quorum members free memberships, all of which were activated. This gave him firsthand insights into their, *er*, personal predilections via their online profiles, which I presume he planned on using against them when the time was right."

Unfortunately Breck's time ran out. Whereas the assassination attempts by his long lost daughter, Edwina Doyle, failed to take out the scumbag munitions magnate, Carl finished him off just as Jack and I were trying to convince him to turn in his Quorum buds.

Carl also exterminated another Quorum member fighting for the top spot, which was vacant since Breck's death. The man was Miles Lardner, a Silicon Valley venture capitalist.

There are now only eleven Quorum members standing.

Abu frowns. "Don't their Sugar CEO profiles give us enough intel to apprehend them?" Abu asks.

"That's the problem. One of the privileges of membership—both in the Quorum, and in Sugar CEO—is that no one knows anyone's real names." Ryan frowns. "Apparently both use the same encryption technology as well, which is why Arnie has yet to break it."

Arnie winces. Like the rest of us, he knows failure is not an option.

I guess this is where I come in. Or not. "Doesn't the term 'sugar baby' imply someone under thirty? Would this be a better mission for Emma?"

Emma chokes on her cream-filled doughnut. "No way in hell! I'm strictly ComInt. Besides, I wouldn't be caught dead with any of those man-ho sleazeoids. What if one of my peeps from the Bust.com community saw me out with one of them? I'd be asked to turn in my membership!"

"Quite frankly, Emma, you're not equipped with the kind of spycraft necessary for this mission." Emma is actually relieved by Ryan's declaration. "Even an experienced honeypot will have her hands full flipping eleven suspects." He turns to me. "Donna, you could pass. You're not even thirty-five yet, am I right?"

I opened my eyes wide so that he'll believe me when I say, "Nowhere near it."

I ignore Jack's coughing fit. He knows I'll be exactly that in a few weeks.

Thank goodness Ryan ignores it, too. Of course, he has no choice. Neither Jack nor Abu look as good in high heels and a push-up bra.

"I would imagine their sugar baby wish list varies a great deal. What makes you think I'll fit any of the descriptions?"

"The Sugar CEO account I've set up for you is riddled with

spiders that mirror the key words found in the suspects' wish lists," Arnie explains. "For example, if one is looking for a blonde working on her masters in English Lit, you're his girl. If another wants a redhead on a swim scholarship who lives in Seattle, *voila*, your profile pops in his email box. At the same time, emails from any other lovely ladies responding to our mystery men will be blocked, so that you're the de facto choice, all courtesy of your favorite computer hacker."

Oh, lucky me. "So that we're all on the same page, are you saying there's to be no exterminations?" I ask.

"As was the case with Breck and Gardner, we need them alive," Jack explains. "Each of them holds a piece of the puzzle to the Quorum's success as an international terrorist organization. Individually, each man has the means to finance it. But it is their collective knowledge and connections—in regard to politics, technology, finance, transportation, munitions, and science—that brought them together in the first place. Not to mention their mutual desire to take down the status quo. The true power is in their synergy. And the secrets they have on each other."

Ryan turns to me. "Once they send you an email requesting a date, Arnie can code a Trojan into your email response, which hacks into their smart phone or computer. That gives us some useful intel, including GPS coordinates and access to his other emails and texts. Granted, there may be some additional decoding needed on their secure files before that methodology helps us determine who they are. Now, as their 'date,' they may be open enough to give you their real names. Even if they don't you'll also be wearing your webcam contact lenses. This allows us to put them through Interpol's facial recognition system. We'll also be putting your conversations with them through voice recognition software. Once a match is made, intel can be gathered almost instantaneously, and we'll feed you a few sound bites regarding his misdeeds that should convince him to turn on his Quorum brethren. One way or another, I know you'll get your man. Or in this case, your men."

Ah, yes, my notorious powers of persuasion. I wish they worked as well on coercing my children to eat their vegetables and brush their teeth.

Or in getting Jack to see his ex, Valentina, for what she really is: a liar.

Good or bad, I'm who I am—an assassin—because of the Quorum. The day I take down that organization, I'll start living the peaceful life I long for: with my children.

And with Jack.

"As soon as I lose this charm bracelet," I lift my leg to make my point, "I'm your woman. I mean, sugar baby.'"

Arnie smiles. "Piece of cake. All I have to do is deactivate it just long enough to swap Emma's ankle for yours."

"'Wow. So, Inga's' back?" I give Emma a thankful nod.

She shrugs. "Yeah, as long as the fridge is full and carpool is covered, so I don't have to deal with your petty neighbors." Emma shudders. Playing a Swedish exchange student isn't her favorite cover, but it's perfect whenever we need her close by.

Still, I'm iffy on a concept that could land me in the clink for the rest of my life. "Won't an interruption in the signal bring the Fed's SWAT team calling?"

Arnie shakes his head. "I can ghost the signal's frequency, for up to three minutes. And it should only take a minute to pick the lock, so that we can replace your ankle with hers."

"In the meantime, I'm pulling every string I can find to clear things up with the Department of Justice," Ryan promises. "But it won't be easy. Remember, they've lost a Gitmo prisoner, and they feel you're their only reasonable lead."

I still can't get the image of Lynch out of my head.

If I succeed, it's to avenge his death, too.

I stare down at my foot, then prop it on the arm of Arnie's chair. "Okay, go for it. Just watch the toes. The paint job is still wet."

CHAPTER 4

HOW TO DRESS FOR SUCCESSFUL DATES

Great first impressions start with good grooming! Before you open your door to your date, wash and style your hair.

Indulge in a mani-pedi.

Put on your face paint, but don't overdo it. The goal is to cover up, not to lay it on thick.

Wear a flattering dress. And certainly put on a pair of heels, since they always make a woman's legs look great, and give her a slimming silhouette.

A bit of jewelry is like feathers on a peacock, drawing a man's eye to the most flattering places: your neck, your wrists, your waist, your hair, and your face.

Surprise! The best accessory of all: a Baby Browning .22 caliber semi automatic. Less than three inches and not even ten ounces, this little gun fits in the palm of your hand (not to mention in a purse, up a sleeve, or in your bra).

With Baby onboard, any gentleman caller who turns out to be no gentleman at all but a slob who likes playing impromptu game of slap-and-tickle will listen when you warn him to move his hand.

Or else lose an eye. Have fun!

"What's your weight?" Jack murmurs.

That's the wrong question to ask a woman as she's wiggling into a Spanx Slim Cognito shape slip. "Um...one-o-nine." I answer him.

Jack's head whips around so fast, you'd think he needs an exorcist. He closes an eye and cocks his head to one side. "For real?"

"Yes, of course!" I turn my back to him, so he doesn't see that my face is as red as a tomato: not because my circulation has been cut off, but from my indignation that he'd have the nerve to question me. "My God, I've been answering these silly questions all night! What does it really matter? According to Arnie, the minute my profile goes live, it will automatically simulate the desired characteristics reflected in the suspects' accounts."

"You know the drill. We still have to fill out the profile fields, or else Sugar CEO won't accept your application. There are just a few more questions, so bear with me. Of course, if you want me to do it without you—"

"Ha! Don't you dare."

"Have a little faith! I promise to follow your lead and fill in a bunch of lies."

While he taps away on the computer keyboard, I rummage through my collection of wigs to see what I can salvage from Trisha's last play date with her best friend, Janie Breck. Thanks to the girls' mutual addiction to sweet pink cotton candy-flavored Bubble Yum, so far three of them need to be shortened or tossed. I hope I have a few left over so that Jack can take pictures of me in them. That way, Arnie's software algorithm will upload the one that best corresponds with the target's sugar baby wish list.

"You're going to have to answer some true/false, comment and multiple choice questions. Okay, question number one: If you had a porn name, what would it be?"

"Ha! I'll just bet they don't ask the sugar daddies the same thing."

"Good supposition. Let me see." He opens another screen and scrolls through the website. "You're right, they don't. But they do ask the dude's net worth, starting at 25 million and going up from there."

"Cha-*ching!* Okay, that evens the playing field somewhat. If I'm going to be someone's fantasy, he's got to make it worth my while. In that case, type in 'Mila Johansson' as my porn name."

"Not fair. All you've done is to combine the names of two very capable actresses."

"It's perfectly fair. Tell me, what were they're last roles?"

"All I remember is that both were squeezed into something sexy."

"You've just proven my point. You noticed nothing about these women, either above their lips or below their knees."

"And the most desirable feature on your sugar daddies will be their bank accounts." Jack snickers as he clicks away furiously on the computer keyboard. Whatever *merde* he's writing, no doubt he's laying it on thick.

"We all play to our strengths. Other than money and temporary security, what else do these jerks have to offer?" I put down the scissors with a sigh. They're useless anyway. Now that I've chopped my favorite auburn wig to shreds, it looks worse than Anne Hathaway's in her *Les Miserables* death scene. "Besides, this mission is quick and dirty, in and out. Prick them with truth serum, which allows Emma to record their answers. Then use the info they give me to turn them, and leave."

He catches my eye in the mirror. "These guys aren't dummies. If they get suspicious, they'll make sure you won't leave their little love nests alive. Their battalion of bodyguards will be right outside the bedroom door."

"Jack, you know I appreciate your concern. I realize I have eleven chances to screw things up. On the other hand, I have eleven opportunities to put the Quorum out of business, once and for all."

"It would have been easier with Carl still behind bars."

"Well, he isn't, and now it's make-up time. And besides, you and Abu will be close by."

He shrugs. "All I'm saying is be careful, okay?"

I nod. "Okay, I promise. Cross my heart. Now, hit me with another question."

"Are you a cat person, or a dog person, and why?"

"Put down 'I love it doggy style.'"

"Don't I know it," he murmurs. "Now, this next question is true or false: I want a relationship with no strings attached."

"Click true."

"Sure," he says, but at the same time he winces. For us, role-playing is a way of life.

And of death.

"Next, another multiple choice: I'd rather be (a) at a disco (b) at the opera (c) cheering courtside at a Lakers game, or (d) sunning myself naked on a beach."

Now it's my turn to frown. "Choose anything but the beach!"

He laughs out loud. "I would have guessed that. Okay, now: If you were a tree, what kind would you be? The choices are (a) Redwood (b) Dogwood (c) Oak, or (d) Japanese Maple."

"Make me a Dogwood."

"Why?"

"Because it's small and the flowers are either pink or white. Subliminally, the message here is 'virginal and girly.'"

"But you're really an Oak, right?"

"Nah. A Redwood. I'm in it for the long run."

He knows exactly what I mean.

"Okay, next up: Would you rather date (a) an artist (b) a banker (c) an entrepreneur or (d) a corporate industrialist?"

"I guess we both know the answer to that one." My eyes seek his out. "I only have eyes for you."

This earns me a knowing smile. "Last question: Where would you prefer to be kissed, and why?"

"Seriously? They ask something that personal?" I slip behind him so that I can read over his shoulder. "They make it quite clear what this is all about, don't they?....Wait! I don't see that question here."

"My bad. It's my question, not theirs." He pulls me into his lap.

Sure, I'll play along. "Want to take a guess?"

He chuckles. "I'm a hands-on kind of guy. How else can I gauge your true enthusiasm?"

He's got a point there.

He hits the SUBMIT button, then forwards Arnie my User ID and password. The photos can wait until our private little survey is completed.

We've only tested six possible kissing locations when Arnie's email pings Jack's computer. We let out with a mutual groan, then disentangle ourselves in order to read it:

You're live, sugar babe!

What Arnie lacks in subtlety, he makes up for with enthusiasm.

"But how can that be?" I ask, "We never sent photos!"

"Heck if I know. Let me test your submission with a fake CEO profile." He opens one, and types in a wish list with the exact profile I submitted.

In no time at all, my profile falls into his email box.

Except that my head now sports long blond hair in coiling tendrils, and has been superimposed onto a body that looks suspiciously like Scarlett Johansson's.

Jack gives a low whistle. "I'm not saying Arnie can improve on perfection, but he sure as hell comes damn close."

I pelt Jack with a pillow.

The next thing we hear is a few bars of "Easy Street" as a Sugar CEO meeting request drops into my Sugar Babe account.

My very first gentlemen caller has come a'knocking.

"It's the bewitching hour," Jack mutters with a sigh.

The rest of the kissable positions on my must-do list will have to wait.

I brace myself before clicking onto it.

Sugar CEO Number 1 claims to be "one of the founders, and chief technical officer of a multi-billion dollar conglomerate."

"Bingo," Jack says.

The sugar baby profile that caught his attention states that I grew up in Chicago, and that currently I am working on my Doctorate in Art History at Columbia, in which I ruminate on the effect of France's political turmoil on the Impressionists painters.

I'm sure the fact that my picture shows a sleek brunette, whose body is busting out of a low-cut ball gown had nothing to do with his interest in me.

Now that I know I'm expected to have Megan Fox's curves (Arnie is proving to be a master at PhotoShop), I've got to squeeze into two more Spanx and a strapless Victoria's Secret Bombshell bra.

His email states that he is looking for "a companion with style and discretion."

"Codeword for 'I've got a wife,'" Jack smirks.

It also says that he was attracted to me because of my love of art. Or as he puts it: "How refreshing to find someone who knows a Monet from a Manet. If you'll allow me, this Saturday evening I'd like to give you a private tour of the American Wing of the Metropolitan Museum of Art. I'm hoping to impress you with my own modest donation to the museum's Hudson River School collection. Shall we say eight o'clock?"

"So, he wants an egghead arm charm," I murmur. "Talk about a change of pace. I guess we better pack a bag for the Big Apple."

"Emma is already here at the house, so the kids have some coverage. Still, perhaps you should call Aunt Phyllis and ask her if she'll stay the weekend, too, in case they need rides to their basketball games."

"God help the good folk of Hilldale," I mutter under my breath. Aunt Phyllis's speeding tickets are bankrupting me.

Jack nods. He knows exactly what I mean. "I'll ask Ryan to set you up with a Gramercy Park address that fits the bill. Then you can write back to CEO Number One."

"I better brush up on late nineteenth century American art. So, who do you like better, Church or Bierstadt?"

"Depends. Which of those dudes painted a better nude?"

I sigh. "Just....never mind."

CHAPTER 5

WHEN AND HOW TO KISS

Kissing is an art form, one which true connoisseurs delight in pursuing!

By the third date, give yourself permission to go beyond the chaste acts of polite conversation and handholding, and allow him to kiss you. Here's how:

First, position yourself next to him. You must be close enough for him to bend forward to kiss you, but not so close that he can't breathe naturally. (That said, for the time being put away the hood and noose, and forego any thoughts of a chokehold.)

Next, pucker up! To do so properly, don't open so wide that he thinks you're about to bite. (Of course you do like a toothy nip now and then, but there's a time and place for everything. He'll know when he's on the receiving end of your incisors, and it won't be pretty). Nor must you open your mouth so slightly that he feels the urge to pry it open with a tire jack. (Albeit, it does give the illusion of chastity. I leave the need for that to your discretion.)

Now, don't be surprised if you find him counting your cavities with his tongue. He's trying to impress you with his knowledge of French: French kissing, that is! Neither of your tongues should feel the urge to (a) tongue wrestle (b) skitter down each other's throats, or (c) stick to the roof of the other's mouth like day-old bubble gum. French kissing is a mouth waltz, a sign of desire, a show of acceptance.

As opposed to his hand up your skirt, since it is thoroughly improper.

Should you find it there, biting is now appropriate: down hard, on his tongue. Without having said a word, he'll certainly get the message; move it, or lose it.

It's been a while since I've been on a real date, one where you're thrilled to learn that someone desires you, and only you, for a few hours. Perhaps for a night. And maybe for the rest of your life.

You adorn yourself in the hope of living up to all his expectations. You put on a dress that clings and flows. And a bra that not only lifts and separates, but plumps, cleaves, and perks you in the direction of the stratosphere. Forget the granny panties. Time for rip-it-off-of-me ass floss. And finally, you strap on high heels that force you to stand up straight, saunter slowly, and topple seductively into his arms.

On the appointed night, you'll flex well-honed skills that entice and allure, like the come hither smile; the wide-eyed admiration; the flirtatious aside. You'll conjure the magic that makes him obsess over you; to want you, and only you, for a lifetime.

For Sugar CEO Number One, I have to be that woman, and more.

He anticipates a woman named Lorelei Saunders, who is in her early thirties, and is well-traveled and well-bred. Lorelei is demure, and can converse on many subjects, but specifically the subject that interests him the most: fine art.

His smile is proof that I live up to his expectations.

As for Sugar CEO Number One, he is balding, slight, and soft-spoken. He is also dressed casually: a black crewneck sweater under an expensive wool herringbone jacket, and Corneliani brogues under tan slacks with razor-sharp creases.

At the appointed time, he greets me on the front steps of the Metropolitan Museum of Art with a gentle kiss on the cheek. When a brisk breeze wraps my sheer, gauzy dress around my thighs, he does the gentlemanly thing and glances away.

Having personally known two Quorum leaders and their best hard man intimately, he isn't at all what I expected. Jonah Breck exuded power and masculinity, but he was also a sadist who raped women, and sold them into slavery. Miles Lardner, the Silicon Valley venture capitalist, was a freewheeling, free spending playboy with a need to be sexually dominated. Both were forced into uncompromising positions (by me) to divulge the Quorum's secrets, but Carl killed them before they were able to do so.

It's a good thing for both of us Carl is now on the run.

Sugar CEO Number One is about twenty years older than me, which means I'm still young enough to have been his daughter, and most certainly younger than the woman he has been married to for the past thirty-three years, and who bore him the three daughters he presumes I'll never find out about.

Wrong. Because he scrutinizes me as openly as I do him, Arnie's facial recognition software is able to place his broad, florid face immediately: "Benjamin Rooney, president and chief technology officer of Bosco Systems," Arnie whispers into my ear. "Bosco supplies the coding technology for the Department of Defense's unmanned missile systems. Rooney is one of the founders, but he chafes under a board of directors that would prefer he take a golden parachute so that they can take the company public, something that would expose his Quorum link, and the revenues it generates."

Well, there you have it. He's got a motive for selling out his company, and he certainly has something important to offer the Quorum.

I note a slight Midwestern accent as he declares, "Tonight I'll be your personal tour guide. Afterward, I've arranged for us to have a private dinner under *Cloud City*, in the roof garden."

I smile. "Ah yes! I've yet to see Tomás Saraceno's masterpiece. I guess VIP membership has its privileges."

He smiles modestly. "You caught me red-handed, trying to impress you."

"Well, you've succeeded."

The guards know him well enough to smile reverently and let us pass by with no more than a deferential nod. The American Wing is on the third and highest floor of the museum. Once here, we are left alone. As we walk through the gallery, I flatter his ego by complimenting his knowledge on such renowned paintings as Thomas Cole's *View of Mount Holyoke*, and John Frederick Kensett's *Lake George*. My own facts are courtesy of MMA's website, which Emma whispers into my diamond stud earpiece.

We stop to admire the thunder clouds roiling over the darkened skies in Martin Johnson Heade's *Newburyport Meadows*. I am making some comment about the shaft of light illuminating one of the haystacks in the painting when he leans in to kiss me.

I freeze for a moment before kissing him back. When he pulls away to gauge his effect on me, I blush.

He squeezes my hand. "You seem like a nice girl. Excuse my bluntness, but in all honesty, it surprises me to find a woman of your caliber trolling Sugar CEO."

I laugh. "And you seem like a nice guy. I guess I could say the same about you."

"Have you heard that old adage, 'It's lonely at the top'? I live it every day of my life."

It will seem lonelier once he hears what I have to say to him.

I've got a saying for him, too: *If you play with fire, you're sure to get burned.*

My face must reflect this thought, because his smile fades. Up until now, everything has been peachy keen. To ensure it stays that way, he puts a hand on the small of my back and leads me toward the elevator at the end of the wing. "You must be famished. Shall we move on to *Cloud City*? I hope you like steak *au pouvre*. It's from my favorite restaurant."

Sure, whatever. Every condemned man is allowed a last meal.

By the time dinner is over, between the worm already planted in his smart phone and the facial recognition ID, we should have the necessary data to convict Mr. Rooney.

I wonder how he'll break the news to the wife whom he no longer loves, and to the daughters who certainly adore him.

When life as you know it goes on life support, it's easy to roll through the five stages of grief:

Denial. Anger. Bargaining. Depression. Acceptance.

For Benjamin Rooney, denial is a blank incomprehensible stare, even when confronted with the specifics of how he's tampered with the codes of two US anti-aircraft missiles aimed at North Korea, so that they are capable of taking down a few of our commercial jets instead. "So, you're not Lorelei Saunders?"

"No, sorry. But my name isn't important. However, the fact

that you are one of the Quorum's leaders means a lot to the US government and many other governments around the globe."

That's when his anger kicks in. "Who the hell do you think you are, accusing me of this crap?" He tosses his napkin on the table and jumps up.

"Mr. Rooney, the moment you try to exit the building, you'll be handcuffed by Federal agents. We already have evidence of your Quorum activity, from your own computer and cell phone."

I pull out my cell, where Arnie has already sent me a screenshot of a decrypted message that Benjamin is sure to recognize: his terms of negotiation with the Quorum, for the North Korean code. "Your only hope of escaping prison is to cooperate fully with us."

His eyes dart from side to side as he feels his world caving in. Depressed, tears stream down his face as he paces the length of the rooftop. "They approached me! They made it seem so easy, so fail-proof—"

"Who is 'they,' Mr. Rooney? Can you in fact identify other members of the organization?"

"Yes....no!...Well, okay, one, maybe. I only met him once. But when they need something, he calls."

"So you can recognize his voice."

"Yes, I guess I can." He buries his head in his hands. "But you don't understand! He'll...he'll kill me!"

"By cooperating, you'll get immunity from prosecution. We can protect you. You and your family will be put in Witness

Protection." I pause then add, "I'm sure you'll want them safe at all costs."

He pauses at the far edge of the roof in order to stare at me. He stands still for so long that I feel he has hardened into one of the Rodin sculptures we just recently admired. *The Head of Sorrow* may be etched in despair, but Benjamin Rooney's frown is deepened by fear.

Finally he nods. "Yeah, okay. Call your people. Tell them I'll talk."

He looks up, as if cursing the heavens over this twist of fate. Twinkling stars blanket the sky above Central Park's vast white gray lawn.

I don't need to reach for my cell. Arnie and Jack already hear all and see all. In fact, they both shout "Shit...he jumped!" into my ear when, like me, they watch Benjamin topple over the side of the roof.

I run to the edge and look over. His head, turned to one side, lies in a pool of dark blood. His body, arms and legs akimbo on concrete, is laid out like an Egyptian hieroglyphic.

In no time at all several people have already gathered around him, including a few MMA security guards, Jack and Abu. Abu blends in because he's also wearing an MMA security guard uniform, while Jack is in one of his expensive suits, as if he's just an upper East Side swell taking a stroll on a mild spring evening.

After the shock of what they see in front of them melts, their eyes instinctively move skyward, toward the roof.

Toward me.

Just as I duck out of sight, I see Abu trying to direct their attention back down toward Benjamin. Playing along, Jack kneels over the body but whispers, "I've pocketed his cell phone. Get out. *Now.*"

I'm already running down the nearest stairwell.

"When you reach the ground floor, head outside. I've disarmed the alarms," Arnie says. "And I'm already erasing the webcam footage of Rooney and his 'date.'"

"Good, because at least two guards saw me with him." Even in wig and contact lenses that are different from my real eye color, a digital video picture would make it easy for someone to place me.

The Feds, for example, who think I'm home in Hilldale under lock and key.

I don't stop until I reach the ground floor. Hearing footsteps, I duck behind a statue just as two guards run past me up the stairwell.

"Take the path around to the left, to the 79th Street Transverse Road," Jack says. "I'll meet you on the corner. Move quickly. The cops and an ambulance are already on the way."

My heart is racing, not because a black-and-white has just passed by or from fear or exertion, but because of my own anxiety over Rooney's death. He seemed sincere about playing ball. In fact, he seemed relieved.

But nothing in life is black or white. No one is all good, or all bad. I got the feeling he was just some guy too smart for his own good, who had found himself in over his head.

I'd done what I could for him. I'd given him a way out from his pact with the devil.

So, why did he choose to jump?

I wish I hadn't been the last person he'd kissed, let alone the last person to see him alive.

CHAPTER 6

HOW TO HANDLE HIS PROMISE, "I'LL CALL YOU..."

The date was fantastic. Sublime. Perfect.

You've given him... what, all of twenty-four hours to contact you for a second date, which will also confirm your gut instinct that the two of you were meant to live together for eternity.... Right?

So why won't he return your calls? (fifteen so far, and counting....)

Was just one date enough for him to make up his mind that he's "just not that into you?"

That is not acceptable.

No time for a pity party! He loves you. He really, really loves you. Here's how to get him to realize his mistake:

First, put a webcam on his house, so you can track his comings and goings, which will allow you to intercept him and ask him, "What the hell? Why haven't you called?"

Next, put a GPS tracker on his car, in case he somehow gets away from you. That way, you can pretend to run into him, allowing you to say, "Wow! Fancy meeting you here... So, why haven't you called me?"

Finally, when he gets the restraining order issued, apply for a legal name change, so that you can keep close to your precious. In time, he'll suck it up and accept what you've known all along:

You complete him.

"Well, that didn't go so well," Ryan says.

Like, duh. "Go ahead, be blunt. Tell me what you really think."

It takes a moment, but finally he gets the fact that I'm joshing with him. He shakes his head. "Not funny, Donna."

"I'm sorry, Ryan. And yes, I get it: I screwed up. I should have turned Benjamin Rooney. Frankly, I thought I'd done just that. When he jumped, I didn't see that coming."

"No need to apologize. I was watching along with you, and it threw me for a loop, too." Ryan rubs his eyes, as if doing so will wipe away his concern over the turn of events. "Well, we should have more luck with the others. In fact, a second Sugar CEO has already contacted you, and not a moment too soon. Emma has picked up some new chatter on Carl. Apparently he's planning a surprise retaliation to prove he's back in full force."

"Do we know where, or when?" Jack asks.

"Emma is trying to connect the dots, but she's had no luck as of yet."

I sigh. "I guess I should get Jeff out of her hair."

Yes, it's true, Jeff has discovered girls. Make that women. Well, one in particular. While he wouldn't be caught dead talking to the giggling ten-year-old hussies who call our house asking for him, he's been panting after Emma since she moved into the bonus room over the garage. Who knew his very first crush would be a kohl-eyed Mohawked nymphet with two nose rings and a penchant for platform boots and tight black leather jeans?

Note to self: Lock son in a closet during teen years.

Second note to self: Do the same for daughters.

Jack laughs when he sees the look of fear on my face. "Relax. Frankly, I think Emma enjoys the attention. She's even taught Jeff how to break simple code."

Arnie turns around to stare at us. It's dawning on him that there's a competitor for Emma's affections.

Dude: you snooze, you lose. Even to a ten-year-old.

I'm still not sure if I should be worried, or pleased. "Well, knock me over with a feather! Unless it's a video game, Jeff's attention span is shorter than that of a gnat."

"In this case, it may play to his favor," Ryan says. "The key to cryptanalysis is frequency analysis. Certain letters of the alphabet appear more often than others. Code breakers recognize the same symbol—or in this case, letter—and work through combinations. The same goes for video gameplay. Repetition is what players look for." He smiles. "Apparently Jeff is a quick learner. A chip off the old block."

Two blocks, in fact. But I'll pass on reminding him that he's Carl's child, too. "If Carl is on the warpath, it's got to be with the Quorum's blessing. Can't we mine Benjamin's cell phone for pertinent intel?"

"Every message Benjamin archived or has received since we hacked his phone has been vetted for originating sources, known contacts, and coded messages. Thus far, we've found no red flags that indicate a covert Quorum missive on the event. Of course, we'll keep monitoring it."

Emma clatters down the stairs, Jeff on her heels. "I've got some news," she interrupts.

All heads turn toward her. Usually this sort of triumph is accompanied by a smile, but today Emma is as grave as a pallbearer.

She's about to speak, but Jeff beats her to the punch. "Whatever it is you're looking for, it's going to happen on Mom's birthday! What are the odds of that? And I was the one who figured it out!"

He looks over at me, waiting for the shower of praise that usually comes from his tiger mom. But all I can offer up is a pat on the back and a shaky smile. That son of a bitch, Carl! Contrary to his twisted way of thinking, making my birthday a national day of mourning is not the ultimate birthday gift.

Jack is perceptive enough to realize my face has lost its rosy hue. He's about to say something, but just then my computer wails the Five song, *Sugar Daddy*.

"Yee-hah!" Arnie shouts. "We've got a live one, folks."

About damn time. I need a distraction from Carl and his sentimental bullshit. Since Jack walked into my life, Carl has been a lover scorned, and he's got one hell of a way to show it.

I'm kidding myself. This isn't about me. It's not even about "we." It's always about Carl, and Carl alone.

Too bad he feels the need to invite the whole world to his pity party.

The email from my second Sugar CEO is filled with sweet teases. Dig it:

"You're a worldly young woman, who will fit in easily at the whirlwind social events that it is my good fortune and privilege to fund and attend.

A typical date with me? Why not join me this Saturday for a private picnic at the Horse Park, in Woodside? Afterward, you'll watch me and my polo team defeat the Argentine national champions. If you're ready to play princess to my Prince

Charming, email back and I'll pick you up: not in a pumpkin carriage, but in my Bentley."

Well, la dee dah.

"At least this guy has dropped a few clues as to who he may be," Jack says. "How many big San Francisco-based corporate honchos who own a string of polo ponies can there be?"

Arnie takes up that challenge. Fourteen keystrokes later he murmurs, "Too many. Try eleven....nope, twelve."

It's nice to see someone is living the dream.

I shrug. "A polo game won't be intimate enough for the conversation I'll be having with him. I'll have to get him talking on the drive over from San Francisco, or during our private picnic. But neither venue makes it easy for me to get him to turn on his fellow Quorum directors. And it certainly doesn't put me front and center with his computer, for validation."

"Arnie, hustle up with a phone app that will do the trick." Ryan turns to me. "To speed things along, you may have to slip him an SP-117 Mickey. That way, we'll have both audio and video admissions of his Quorum activities. After you've given him the anecdote, he'll feel refreshed, but he won't remember a word he said—that is, until you reel off his indiscretions, perhaps when you're alone with him again, after the match. That should convince him to cut a deal."

Jack puts his arm around my waist. "Abu and I will trade off on surveillance, both on the road and on the polo grounds. As backup, plant an audio-enhanced GPS microdot somewhere in the back seat, where it won't be detected. That way, we can listen in after he drops you off. It'll be interesting to hear whom he calls first, after you've turned the screws on him."

I know who Jack is thinking of: Carl.

If so, we'll be able to trace the call and capture him.

Then I can go back to living a normal life. Like other women, my family is not just a valid excuse to give up my day job, but a noble one as well.

But isn't my assassination vocation just as noble? Or is it futile? Let's face it, there will always be bad guys. I can't shoulder this burden forever.

I want to watch my kids grow up. I want to be there when they go off to college, get married, and have children of their own.

I want Jack at my side, forever.

Until death do us part.

The next time he hears that line, I want him to think of what he has with me, not what he lost when Valentina walked out of his life.

"Does champagne make you tipsy?" Sugar CEO Number Two sounds hopeful as he holds a bottle of Tattinger's over my glass.

I reward him with a shy smile. "It's fun to lose control every now and then, don't you agree...Richard?"

As if. I'm beginning to believe that "control" is this guy's middle name. It's anyone's guess as to his last name, or any other clue as to his identity.

On the hour ride from San Francisco to Woodside I had very little success getting him to talk about what he did for a living. And no matter how many ways I tried to get him to reveal his last name or his job, he played it coy. "All that corporate bullshit will bore you to tears, sweetheart. Let's just keep things friendly."

By "friendly," he means allowing his hands to cup my breasts while he probes my molars with his tongue.

I've no doubt he presumes I'm the dessert after the gourmet meal of filet mignon, broccoli stir-fry and mashed potatoes, which we ate in a private tent overlooking Woodside California's polo fields. But now our little picnic is almost over. I've only got another half hour before Richard leaves me for a white Arabian mare named Pure as Driven Snow.

To keep him here, I'll have to be anything but.

Even now Arnie whines, "He's much too close for our facial recognition software to get a good fix on his features. Can't you get him to back off?"

"Sure she can," Jack mutters, "by putting her heel in his groin."

Wishful thinking on both our parts. Alas, that would defeat the purpose.

Since I got into the car, Emma and Arnie have been working furiously to place him. But who knew San Francisco had so many steely-eyed mid-fortysomething corporate bigwigs named

"Richard," who are six feet tall, just gray enough around the edges, and own a polo team?

As if reading my mind, Emma murmurs into my diamond-studded audio feed, "We've narrowed down the list of potential suspects to five."

Really? That many?

Time's a'wasting. I toss back the flute of bubbly. Then slowly I run my tongue over my lips and murmur, "Aren't you going to join me?"

Richard sighs. "Believe me, I wish I could. But if I'm going to ride without falling off my horse, I should hold off until after the match."

I give him a playful pout. "It's no fun getting tipsy all by myself." I brush against him when I reach into the picnic hamper. Pulling up another champagne flute, I whisper, "One tiny little sip won't knock you off your horse, will it?"

He eyes both the glass and me longingly. Finally he nods. "I guess you're right."

I take the bottle from his hand. "Let me do the honors. As much as I love being treated like a queen, today I'd prefer to play handmaiden. "

That raises a smile on his face, not to mention a tent in his polo breeches.

I'm sure it also helps that, when I pour the champagne into his glass, I arch my back in such a way that my vee-neck blouse drops between my breasts.

While his eyes are otherwise occupied, I watch his face for Arnie's sake, praying now that I'm just close enough for him to get a lead on the guy. At the same time, I slide the jade stone on my ring and tilt it so that a dose of SP-117 pours into his glass.

He gulps down the champagne. Good, because the sooner his opens up, the better. I keep up the small talk, complimenting him on topics he's already deemed safe: the filet mignon; his Bentley; his polo skills; the size of his biceps beneath his polo shirt; the size of the tent in his breeches—

Until, finally, his eyes glaze over. That's when I know it's safe to ask, "So, tell me Richard, what's your last name?"

"Higginbotham." The word comes out in a drowsy whisper.

"Nailed him," Arnie and Emma yell into my ear at the same time. She adds, "That name was on one of my possible five—" at the same time in which Arnie declares, "The face recognition analysis came through, finally—"

I close my eyes and shake my head. "One at a time, children, please!"

"He's CEO of Catalyst Industries!" Emma's answer comes out in a rush. "It's a conglomerate that owns—"

"—A variety of biotech companies," Arnie interjects, "including, Human-A-Sphere, a chain of bio-genetic profiling labs; Inject-A-Life, a firm that invents non-invasive surgical procedures; and PharmFarm, the largest agribusiness of genetically enhanced crops."

"Any one of those could provide a terrorist organization with the means to cripple a nation." Jack's voice is emotionless as he states this simple fact.

It's time for some answers from the man in question. "Richard Higginbotham, are you a member of the Quorum?"

He nods. Whereas that gives visual affirmation, I want to hear it from his lips. "Answer the question out loud," I prod him.

"Yes, I am one of the Quorum Thirteen...well, now we are eleven...Um, ten." By his frown, I can tell he's surprised to hear himself say this out loud, and to a perfect stranger.

"And what do your companies do for the Quorum?"

"Each of them is developing a component for an ethnic bioweapon."

"What the hell is that?" Emma asks.

"The theory is that ethno-bombs can be used to target specific genetic or cultural anomalies recognized in certain ethnic groups," Arnie explains. "An organic example is how white settlers in the US almost wiped out a tribe of indigenous natives with small pox."

Emma lets loose with a piercing whistle. "I can only imagine how the Quorum plans on using this. Sell it to the highest bidder? Blackmail a government?"

"Try all of the above," Jack says.

"How soon before this project reaches completion?" I ask.

Richard smiles up at me. "We're beta-testing now. I'll be presenting my findings to my Quorum brethren at our next meeting. If it is chosen for implementation, I'll be poised to be the Quorum's next leader."

"Where and when is the meeting?"

"We've yet to receive that information."

"Who are your fellow Quorum members?"

He shrugs. "We never meet without masks. Anonymity allows us to contribute freely, without threat of exposure. "

"Richard, why are you doing this, even when you know it's illegal, unethical, and inhumane?" I have to ask, and not just because I'm incredulous at his despicable behavior, but to get it on record.

He stares at me, as if I'm crazy or something. "For the money, of course! Not just for the fees to our companies, but because of the dividends to thirteen stockholders of Quorum Ltd." He chuckles. "Well, for the ten who are left."

"Donna, unfortunately you don't have time to read him the riot act," Jack says. "So give Sleeping Beauty his wake-up potion and promise you'll rendezvous with him after his match."

"Will do." I pocket Richard's phone. Then I mix the SP-117 anecdote into Richard's champagne flute with a pinky finger and hand it to him. "Here, drink this."

He gulps it down.

When Richard comes to, he's pleasantly surprised to find me straddling him. As I rise, smoothing the skirt of my dress back into place. "Was it as good for you as it was for me?"

To bring him to the right conclusion that we're both satisfied with our little picnic hank-panky, I guide his hand to the clasps on the front of my bra.

He gets the hint, and hooks them into place. "Um....yeah...great!" He smiles, but he shakes his head, confused.

After a long kiss, I help him buckle his breeches. He groans ecstatically as I pat Bobby Junior back into position and shove him toward the tent door. "Why don't we have another go-round, after the match? But only if you're the victor! I'll be cheering from the sidelines, so make Mama proud!"

Richard stumbles out of the tent like a man with the world at his feet. Still, I have no doubt that, presented with his own confession, he'll turn on his Quorum brethren. If not, those feet will be in shackles for the rest of his life.

And I know for a fact that they don't have a polo team in Gitmo.

By the second chukker, Richard's team is up by a goal, thanks to a sixty-five-yard penalty shot by the man himself. He's riding that poor horse like a man who's used to having his way with the fillies.

A guy can dream, can't he?

And a gal can have her nightmares. For me, it comes when suddenly Pure as Driven Snow bolts upright, then slams back down to earth, twisting her front right fetlock and landing on her cannon bone.

Richard summersaults off the mare and breaks his neck.

Pure as Driven Snow lies on her side, wailing her pain in snorts and whinnies.

A few feet away, Richard lies on his stomach, his head wrenched to one side. He eyes the hushed spectators with an unblinking death stare. A crimson halo of blood darkens the verdant turf under his head.

I'm officially two for two. If this keeps up, I'm going to have a very bad reputation as a first date.

Sobs from the crowd rouse the medics into action, Abu among them. Jack takes my hand and pushes me through the crowd.

Our route away from the polo field takes us by Richard's love tent. Jack grabs the picnic basket. We are now just like any other couple, out for a stroll.

If only that were the case.

Neither of us says anything until we get to Jack's car. He's about to put the key in the ignition when we hear a shot: Pure as Driven Snow has been put out of her misery.

Lucky girl.

"Jack, let me ask you a question."

"Shoot...I mean—"

Despite his poor choice of words, we both know what he really meant. "Tell me the truth. Was I a really bad first date?"

He thinks for a moment. "Bad? Nah. Truly lousy, maybe."

"We went to the Sand Dollar, remember?"

He nods. "Great view from that outside deck."

"And the food was awesome. Can't go wrong with a great piece of salmon."

"Agreed. The fish there is always out of this world."

I look down at my hands in my lap. "That night, we had our first dance, as I recall."

"To that slow song, the sultry one. You move really well, you know?"

"You lead, I follow. That's how it works."

He nods at the compliment, but keeps his gaze straight ahead. He still doesn't know where I'm going with this.

"Be honest, Jack. Am I a lousy first date?"

He winces, as if the memory is giving him a splitting headache. "Let me see. You walked out on me while we were dancing—"

"But only because you accused me of being angry at Carl for dying on me!"

"And you stormed out of the car when I tried to kiss you."

"We were interrupted by one of your many girlfriends. She was tossing pebbles at your bedroom window, remember?"

"Can I help it if I'm popular?"

"Can I help it that I refuse to put up with a player?"

His kiss is as it should be, full of passion and promise.

Just like our very first kiss: in front of my children, when we found him coming out of my bathroom. He was a stranger to all of us. And yet, my children welcomed him with open arms. They felt protected immediately.

It has taken me much too long to admit to myself that I do, too.

I pull away slightly, but only to take note that he's hasn't keeled over.

Yep, he's still alive. And he's all mine.

CHAPTER 7

FIVE TELLTALE SIGNS HE WANTS A COMMITMENT

(Or that Perhaps He Wants YOU Committed)

Congratulations! It's now obvious that he wants to be your one-and-only, for the rest of his life! Here's how you know:

First, when you secure all exits so that he can't escape, he doesn't freak out. Instead, he says, "Honey, let's talk through your feelings."

Next, when you waterboard him, it only takes two dunks before he gives the safety phrase, "I can't live without you!"

And finally, he jumps at the chance at getting a big old heart with your name on it tattooed on his bicep. (Granted, it beats the alternative: having it branded on his ass.)

Now Arnie is practically living at the house, too. He claims it's needed so that Emma can do sweeps of the text messages found on Benjamin Rooney and Richard Higginbotham's smart phones, but my guess is that he's afraid Jeff is moving in on his turf.

A ten-year-old? Really? Gimme a break. Spies are a paranoid group. For that matter, so are immature techies.

Not to mention Arnie is just another mouth to feed, which is why I've sent Jack to the Hilldale Whole Foods, to stack up on vittles. This mission is costing us a mint, what with Emma's strict adherence to a vegan diet.

The only good news is that Jeff is eating healthier in order to impress her, unlike Arnie, who slips out to his car every so often to snag one of the Twinkies he's hidden in the trunk.

He slams it quickly when he sees me walk out to get the mail, but the proof that he's feeding his heartache is the cream on his lips. I swipe the back of his hand across his mouth. When he sees the smear, he shrugs. "What does it matter? She doesn't even know I'm here."

"Don't kid yourself. She's quite aware of you. She's just waiting for you to make your move."

His jaw drops halfway to his chest. "Wow. Really? Is that what you think?"

"Arnie, I don't think. I know. So, why don't you ask her out on a date?"

"I...I guess I could." While he contemplates this exotic notion, he stuffs the Twinkie wrapper into the pocket of his sagging jeans. "What do you think, a meal and a movie?"

"Sure, that's a start. Yelp up a five-star vegan joint. Afterwards, take her to a foreign flick. Maybe something German and existential."

He frowns. "You don't think I could talk her into heading over to Chili's for some baby back ribs, then the *Star Wars* retrospective in Culver City?"

"You're trying to impress her, not gross her out." Seeing the devastated look on his face, I quickly add, "It's okay to have different tastes. Opposites attract, yada yada. But if you really want Emma to see you in a different light, you're going to have to show her you're willing to get out of your comfort zone."

"I get it." He sighs. "I figure if it worked for Sarek Xtmprszntwlfd and Amanda Grayson, it can work for Emma and me."

"Say what?"

"Spock's parents. You know, in *Star Trek*. His father is a cool-headed Vulcan, while his mom is an Earthling."

It's times like these I want to smack this boy silly. However, bitch-slapping an Acme asset will only put me in Dutch with the boss man, so instead I give him a shove in the direction of the house. "Do it now, before Jeff gets home from school and tries to impress her by shooting twenty baskets in a row."

It works for all the little mean girls in his class, so he's trying it on Emma. Yes, he's as clueless as Arnie. But in his defense, of course, he's yet to hit puberty.

"You see what I mean? I can't compete against a jock, no matter their age!" Arnie rambles back into the house, and just in time, the lucky duck. Penelope, Tiffy and Hayley drive up, catching me like a deer in headlights. As I rack my brain for an excuse I can give them for whatever torture they've hatched for me, Hayley waves me over with a white envelope.

"Donna, this was delivered to my house, but it seems to be yours," she shouts.

I guess the only way to shut her up is to do it with my fist in her mouth, so I head over her way. "What exactly is it?"

"I don't know. Something from Carl, perhaps?" She holds it up to her nose and sniffs it. "Smells like him: you know, Old Spice. And it's addressed to 'My Darling Donna.' But the 'o' in your name is shaped like a heart, so my guess is that it's a love letter."

What the heck? From Jack?

I snatch it out of her hand. "Hey, this envelope has been opened!"

Tiffy shrugs. "That's what happens when those things get too close to a steam iron."

"Ah, I see." She's lucky I'm not holding one now, because the cord would be wrapped around her pretty little neck.

"Go ahead, read it," Penelope says impatiently. "It'll make your day. I know it made mine. That husband of yours should be writing erotica!"

I'm too dazed to stop her from grabbing it back from me and reading it out loud:

Miss me, Doll?

So sorry I haven't gotten back to you before now, but you know how it is when I'm on the road. It's work, work, work and no play for your man Carl.

That's okay. The "play" part comes the next time you're in my arms.

In fact, I've been doing a lot of thinking about us. Or more specifically, you. About the cute way you always moan during our love play. How your nipples harden at the sight of me. How you always insist on being on top. How all that tough girl naughty talk makes you so damp, and makes me so hard.

And how you do your damnedest to bring me to my knees.

But face it, Donna: more than anything, you love being dominated.

Well, I aim to please. Next time we're together I'll have you writhing in pain, screaming for mercy and begging for me to put you out of your misery.

Sounds like fun, doesn't it?

Soon, my love. Much sooner than you think.

Carl

PS: You are my greatest escape. For that alone I'll always love you.

Why, that son of a bitch!

Give me a break. Everyone moans when they're being strangled. And if I'm damp when I'm with him, it's from perspiration, not passion. Taking down a six-foot-two one-hundred and ninety-five-pound bully is hard work.

And the only reason my nipples are hard when he's around is because I keep my bullets in my bra. No man expects to find cold hard steel next to a warm heart.

The next time we're together, we'll see who ends up writhing in pain.

Carl knew that putting this letter in Penelope's hands would make me the laughingstock of the neighborhood.

Or the most envied woman in Hilldale.

This is all too obvious when Jack's Lamborghini careens up the driveway and he jumps out, two bags of groceries in tow. I know just what Penelope and her posse are thinking: Jack has been catapulted into that rare firmament known as Super Stud Muffin: a husband who not only boasts a Goslingesque physique and pens naughty love notes to his wife, he handles the grocery shopping, too.

Jack has reached my side just as their collective sigh crescendos into something akin to a group orgasm. Waving at his fan club, he murmurs, "What did you do to put them in such pain?"

"That's not pain. It's sheer ecstasy. And I didn't get them

there. You did. Or more to the point, Carl."

Before he has a chance to ask me exactly what I mean by that, the dulcet tones of *Sugar Daddy* chimes from my cell phone.

I've got another date with destiny.

As Jack nudges me toward the front door, I can just imagine what my neighbors are thinking: once again, the Stones are in for an evening of fun and games.

If only they knew.

I'm already inside the house when I realize Penelope still has Carl's letter. I guess I'll have to break into the Bing household in order to get it back.

My guess is that I'll find it in her nightstand drawer, next to her dildo.

My latest invitation reads this way:

"I prefer a bird like you, who doesn't mind carrying a little meat on her bones. It's a pleasant change for a toff like me self, who's tired of watching pretty women turn up their noses at a savory steak and kidney pie, or take a bite or two, only to boak it all out in the loo. If you're thinking to yourself, 'This bloke is too right,' I say let's quit twatting around and hit the trough together, my treat.

In fact, my private chef will create a fantasy feast fit for milady. Your obsessive predilection for 'greasy bangers' (as you so delightfully put it) has been duly noted, and is much appreciated. Expect my limo outside your flat by 1800 GMT."

Interesting. "I take it, then, we're off to jolly ol' London?"

"Righto." Jack taps away on his iPad, arranging our Acme jet. "I guess this sugar daddy is something of a foodie."

"If so, then maybe I should wait to break the news to him after dessert, so that I get a square meal. In US currency, Acme's per diem sucks. In London, we won't be able to afford chips with our fish."

"I hear ya, sister."

While he makes our arrangements, I click onto the profile that got my latest mate all hot and bothered. It's not a pretty site. My face has been PhotoShopped to look forty pounds heavier. It now sits on a body that looks suspiciously like Melissa McCarthy's.

Underneath, the caption reads, "I'm a slag for a platter of bangers and mash!"

Right now the only thing I want on a platter is Arnie's head. "Arnie! Get your ass in here!"

Both my Smith & Wesson and a Beretta are within reach. After this bit of chicanery, Arnie should be so lucky that I aim at his feet and not his kneecaps.

Jack is fully aware of this. "Whoa, cowgirl! You can't shoot the boy wonder."

"Oh no? Why not?"

"He's an Acme asset." When he realizes a shrug is all he'll get from me, he adds, "Besides, if he pees on your rug, you'll have one big mess on your hands."

Damn it, cooler heads always prevail.

"No way in hell am I beefing up for this gig," I grumble.

"I hear you, loud and clear. Okay, so when the guy sees you, tell him that since your profile went up, your doctor insisted you go on the Mediterranean Diet." He pulls me into his lap for a kiss. "Besides I like you just the way you are."

"Oh, yeah? How is that?"

Jack knows a trap when he hears one. "Um... you know, just right. Perfect, in fact."

"Not plump?"

"You? Nah!"

"Zaftig, maybe?"

He tilts his head as he contemplates an answer that will keep all his fingers and toes intact. "I may not know how to spell that, but I'm smart enough to know I should say no."

That's my boy.

Unlike, Arnie, who has a lot of explaining to do. When he doesn't show up, I realize the tone of my voice tipped him off that he's now persona non grata in the Stone hacienda. He's headed back to Acme headquarters.

That's okay. I know where he lives.

The London apartment Acme has secured for me is in a shabby chic walk-up in the boho neighborhood of Notting Hill.

As agreed, Sugar CEO Number 3's limo driver rings the bell promptly at eight o'clock in the evening. This is a hired ride, so there is no reason to leave a GPS bug on the back seat for future tracking. Besides, my earring will track and transmit my location and any conversations.

The windows are tinted, and I've been blindfolded, so I can't see where we're headed, but Jack and Abu are trailing the limo. When the limo finally pulls to the curb, it turns out we haven't gone too far: just a mile, south and east, to the street known as Kensington Palace Gardens, where every home on the block is really an estate worth tens of millions of pounds, and every neighbor is in fact a billionaire, an ambassador, or a rock star with money to burn.

Life doesn't get better than this.

I'm wearing a raw silk Cavalli dress that flows like a baby-doll negligee. It's low cut, and mini in length. I presume my mystery date expects a muumuu, but this is the best I can do.

Finally the car stops. The driver opens the back door, walks me up the stairs, where two bodyguards stand in front of a heavy oak double doorway. As we approach one speaks sotto voce, which is apparently loud enough to be heard by the mike in his Bluetooth. A moment later the door opens, and I'm ushered in by an elderly butler.

"Please, follow me," the butler murmurs.

"The address has been blinded in the public record," Arnie says. "I can't pull the owner's name. I'll see if I can hack the City of London's property registry."

"Make it quick," Jack warns him.

There are two more guards at attention in the marble foyer rotunda. I'm sure Jack and Abu are taking a headcount, since I may need a little help getting out of here.

Three hallways spoke out from the foyer. We head down the center one, passing one stately room after another until we come to a grand formal dining room.

By the look of things, Henry the Eighth is back, and he's holding a victory banquet. There are dishes of onion with shaved black truffles, a veal tenderloin with a béarnaise sauce, a banana cream pie, oysters on the half shell, whole baked chickens, a rack of lamb, mashed potatoes, a bowl of caviar, a glazed duck, even a lobster.

I'm glad this dress doesn't have a belt.

At least this time I'm not wearing Spanx.

The butler pulls out a chair. I take it I'm supposed to sit down. Okay, works for me.

What I don't count on is his strapping me into arm restraints, and putting a blindfold over my eyes.

"Not good," Jack whispers in my ear. "Now, just how are we going to recognize our man?"

I'm just about to answer when a voice behind me says, "My word! You're not at all what I was expecting! You can't be more than seven stone thirteen."

I do the conversion in my head. That's around one-hundred-and-eleven pounds. Really? I look that heavy to this guy?

Blimey, he hit it right on the head.

"You're pretty good," I say with a sexy murmur. "How about taking off this blindfold, so that I can see you, too."

"No no no, my wispy little sylph! First a little appetizer, to fatten you up! Open up and say, 'Ah.'"

The voice is so close now, I can smell his breath. Pickled herring? Ewwww, yuck. If he sticks that in my mouth, I'll gag, I swear.

I feel his fingers on my lips. When I open them, he crams something between them.

I'm prepared to spit the crap out. But hey, it's pretty darn good. "Yummy! Is that a peach trifle, with a hint of lemon?"

"Yes, sweets for my sweet! Do you like it?"

"To die for. You must give me the recipe."

"You'll have to settle for this." Sugar CEO Number Three tips my nose with something creamy.

I stick my tongue out and up as far as it will go. Alas, not as far as I'm sure Sugar CEO Number 3 would appreciate. No matter. He dabs a little on my lips.

I smack them together. "Whipped cream, with just a hint of

mocha?"

"Ooooh, you're good, my little Yankee Doodle noodle."

He sticks a creamy finger in my mouth. My gag reflex is in full force but I tamp it down and do my best impression of a woman in the throes of an foodgasm.

He must believe I'm turned on because the next thing I know he's slapping something cold, wide, and wet on my décolleté. "Um...excuse me, are those lasagna noodles?"

"Yes. You'll love the sauce! Pesto!"

So much for my designer Cavalli. The only saving grace is that he pulls it off, over my head.

"Oh my God," Arnie gasps, "The dude's a WAMer!"

"A what?" Abu asks.

"He has a food fetish," Jack explains. "WAM is an acronym for 'wet and messy.' As in any kind of food that can be licked off another person."

Abu and Arnie are laughing so hard in my ear that I have to keep from wincing, let alone telling them to shut the fuck up.

"You know, I have a fantasy, too," I purr to Sugar CEO Number Three.

"Do tell, milady."

"I'm lying on this table, naked except for my heels. You can only imagine what I can do with your trifle. Among other things."

His hand pauses on one breast. Next, I feel the restraints come off my wrists. Finally the blindfold comes off, too.

And I'm staring at Britain's answer to Jabba the Hutt. In a tux no less.

Yeah, okay, what did I expect? Calories in and in, and in, equal pounds on. Do the math.

I hold out a dainty hand. "We haven't met formally. I'm Cookie Lonergan. And you are?"

"Hungry," he hisses. He bends down over my breasts, the better to lap up the pesto sauce. "Your name is.... *delicious*."

"I need him looking at you, not drooling on you," Arnie mutters. "Otherwise, the system can't recognize him. I hope his face isn't covered in sauce, or that might make it harder, too."

"Thank God she's not wearing a wire," Abu snickers. "He would have eaten it by now."

I jerk Jabba's head up by the roots of his hair. "My, you've got the most beautiful eyes." I lick my lips. "They're the color of chardonnay grapes. Speaking of which, how about a little wine? You know, something to whet our appetites for our meal?"

"Jolly good idea! We can do it the Japanese way. I'll drink mine out of your golden triangle. Delicious!"

The next thing I know, Jabba is tossing a few of the dishes on the floor and I'm being lifted onto the table. All I can do is pray that Arnie's facial recognition software kicks in, or I'm so greasy that I can slip out of his big paws before I'm his main course.

"He's Baron Maynard McChesney of Whitefriars," Arnie declares triumphantly. "He owns the United Kingdom's largest media conglomerate, including two tabloids, and the country's largest financial newspaper. Rumor has it he's got dirt on every UK celebrity as well as every member of Parliament, and even a few secrets stashed away on the royal family."

"If so, he can blackmail a few pawns who will be valuable for the Quorum," Jack says. "Donna, he should be easy to turn, because he's got so much to lose: wealth, his company, prestige, contacts—"

"Not to mention prison chow is nothing like this," Abu pipes in. "Go get'em, Cookie."

I'm just about to read Maynard the riot act when there's a knock on the door. He sighs, annoyed that he's been interrupted from the task at hand: slathering pesto sauce on my thighs. As he lumbers toward the door, he wipes his hand on a napkin.

"Ah! The *piece de resistance* has arrived!" When he returns to the table, he has a soup tureen with him. "It's my favorite, turtle. Care for a bowl?"

I tamp down the bile rising in my stomach before murmuring, "I'll pass. In fact, this little party is over."

He has different thoughts on the subject. He shoves me onto the table, face down. The soup is hot. He drizzles some up my spine and around my bum and shoulders. When I shudder, he slaps me back down. "You mustn't move, my dear. Not to worry! Daddy will lap it all up."

I struggle, but he's too damn big for me to fight off. And quite frankly, his tongue on my spine is somewhat ticklish and it's making me giggle.

Is he laughing, too? It sounds as if that may be the case.

No, he's gagging on something.

Spasming, really. I hear him gurgle, then sigh.

Then...nothing. All three hundred or more pounds of him flop on top of me.

Make that twenty-one stones. At least!

"Baron, wake up and get off! Now!" I try to jerk myself up, but his dead weight is holding me against the table.

"He's dead?" I hear the dread in Jack's voice. Then: "Aw, damn, a heart attack? Just our luck! Listen, Donna, shimmy out from under him, and get the hell out of there, now."

"Yeah, okay, thanks for that." I squirm to the left, then to the right, but big boy is simply not budging.

"Smear yourself with the mint jelly," Abu suggests. "It may be slippery enough to get you out from under him."

At this point, I'll try anything. I take a handful out of the bowl, and wedge my hand between me and the dead man, then slather it up and down my back.

That does the trick. I inch my way out from under him. I slip back into my dress, which now looks like a Jackson Pollock canvas, and smells like the kitchen sink at an Italian trattoria.

"How the hell are you getting out of there?" Arnie asks.

"Something tells me that many a sugar baby has taken a walk of shame from the baron's abode. Alas, I'll be the last."

"Try to lock the door behind you," Jack says. "I'm sure his

staff knows better than to interrupt him at feeding time. They may lose an arm or something."

"Then I guess he never sees them at all. Did you see that spread?" Abu's tone is dripping with sarcasm, unlike me, who is dripping in pesto, mint jelly and turtle soup.

Green has never been my color.

Turns out I'm right about the Baron's love life. The guards don't give me a second glance.

I walk, make that run, away from the estate. When I turn the corner, Jack and Abu are already waiting for me.

As I hop in, Jack says, "What? No doggy bag?"

Always the smart ass.

CHAPTER 8

IS HE A PLAYER?

Before you fall in love with the new man in your life, ask yourself: does he have what it takes to be true blue to you?

He doesn't if these clues ring true:

Clue Number 1: Whenever you call him, you hear women giggling in the background, along with heavy breathing and gasps: either his, or someone he calls "Doll" when he thinks he's muzzled the phone and you can't hear him.

Clue Number 2: He takes other women along on your dates, who he claims are his sisters. Not only do they look nothing like him, they take turns snuggling him and sitting on his lap;

Clue Number 3: When you finally permit him to ravish you, he insists this passionate act take place at "his sisters' home, because they have a bed large enough for some real fun." The real fun he means comes in the form of the sister act, which is already on said bed, in various states of dishabille.

Clue Number 4: Soon he's introducing you to another woman, he refers to you as "my little sis." Um, no. You have a different kind of relationship with your real brother, one in which swapping spit only happened before the age of twelve, and from a distance of six feet, as opposed to in each other's mouths.

Now, taken together, these clues point to one very important thing: this is not the sort of family you want to marry into, so run away as quick as you can. Take my word for it, he'll be too busy tongue tussling with his supposed sisters to realize you're no longer there.

"Donna, I think you need to sit down for this." Ryan's voice is calm, but since he walked through the door he's been pacing my dining room floor, which is not a good sign.

I freeze from tossing crap into the three Welcome to Hilldale baskets I'm making as part of my Penelope penance. "Oh, heck! Did Reynolds find out I've been AWOL?"

"Thank goodness, no. But—" he pauses to take a deep breath. "The deaths of your Quorum dates weren't accidents."

Emma and Arnie both look up. "Well, the first one was a suicide, so technically it wasn't an accident," Arnie reminds him. "And the third one was a heart attack, so that doesn't count either—"

"Arnie, zip it! The point I'm trying to make is that Donna's dates were murdered." Ryan shakes his head in despair. "The first man—Benjamin Rooney—was shot with a high-powered air rifle. It hit him broadside, and spun him off the roof. The assassin must have been in one of the high apartment buildings, right across the street from the museum. As for Richard Higginbotham, the assassin took down the horse first, in the same manner. He took a second shot, right to the heart, the moment he fell."

Emma's eyes open wide. "But no one could have shot Mayor McCheese—I mean, Maynard McChesney. He and Donna were alone."

"The soup contained aconite. Unless the coroner suspected otherwise, it looked like a heart attack. Acme's autopsy picked it up because we specifically tested for it."

I slump down in my chair. "Well, that certainly explains a lot! I mean, what are the odds that three men would all die on a first date?

"One in 54,302,239, in fact," Arnie pipes in. "But if it's any consolation, your odds decrease by thirteen percent each year, between now and when you're eighty-five. Old codgers keeling over on dates are more prevalent."

"Great to know." Not. "And after eighty-five?"

Arnie looks perplexed. "I didn't calculate beyond that, because it's a long shot that by then any man will even look in your direction." Instinctively he ducks below my couch.

He's lucky I'm too upset to bother throwing anything at him.

The truth of the matter is that I'm worried about Jack. On the plane ride home, he was silent, a telltale sign that he's also concerned about how things have gone down. This morning he left the house before I woke up. His note said he was dropping off two welcome baskets.

But why is it taking him so long to get home?

"I've got more bad news." Ryan puts his hand on my shoulder. "The DOJ refuses to rescind your house arrest order."

"By that, you mean Reynolds still insists I'm one of the bad guys, right?" I crumple tissue paper and stuff it between a bag of cashews, a Hilldale welcome bear, and some homemade jam. If Reynolds were here now, I'd stuff it where the sun doesn't shine.

"Well, yes. He's made an excellent case to his higher-ups that you may in fact be a flight risk."

"The man is crazy! I've got three kids, I'm divorcing Carl, I'm in a loving relationship, and I've got high-security status. What part of my dossier reads 'terrorist moll'?"

"Even if that's the case, you make great bait." Jack's voice comes from directly behind me. Arnie, Emma, Ryan, Abu and I turn toward him at the same time.

Emma shrugs. "Jack's right. If you remember, it's how we resurrected Carl in the first place."

By the look on Jack's face, I imagine Ryan has already given him the bad news about the assassin shadowing our dates with the Quorum. Even before I open my mouth, he knows what I'm going to ask, and he shakes his head. "We've picked up a shadow. At the same time we can't forget we've got a serious enemy in Reynolds."

I'm so angry that I rip a stack of fifty-percent-off local merchant coupons in half. "In other words, I'm the worm in Reynolds's fish hook?"

Ryan shakes his head. "You've wiggled off that hook three times already and he hasn't noticed, thanks to Emma subbing for you, and Arnie watching the FBI surveillance team."

"Damn it!" I run to the window and peek out. Yep, there's one now. Like, a white Ford Fiesta wouldn't be conspicuous in a neighborhood where the most prevalent car is black BMW sedan? Give me a break. "How long have they been out there?"

"I spotted them the day we got back from the polo match," Jack says.

"They've got three shifts going, twenty-four seven," Arnie adds. "But I came up with a way to keep them distracted while you were out of town."

"Oh yeah? How was that?"

"Every night Emma would slap on her 'Donna' wig and put on one of your nightgowns in front of the sheers in your master bedroom window."

Seeing my surprise, Emma turns red as a beet. "Oh, I don't do anything, you know, lewd...Okay, maybe once I flashed a dude. But that was only because I felt sorry for him. He seemed bored out of his gourd. Besides, he's kind of cute."

Arnie frowns. He's not too happy that his great idea backfired.

"If someone else is after the Quorum, we can't lead the

assassin to another Sugar CEO, because he'll murder that guy, too," I say.

Jack smiles. "If Mohammed can't come to the mountain, perhaps the mountain can come to him."

Arnie looks at him, clueless. "I don't get it."

"Up until now, we've been waiting for them to contact Donna," Jack explains. "Instead, why don't we contact them and invite them to an event they wouldn't want to miss?"

Emma snickers. "That should be easy. All we'd have to say is that sex is involved."

"Wow," Arnie murmurs. "Talk about the ultimate Quorum-palooza!"

I shake my head. "Nope, I don't think so! As much as I'd like to get away from all these kinky blind dates, I've got to draw the line at an orgy."

Jack laughs. "That's not exactly what I had in mind. If we word the invitation correctly, they'll all be expecting an intimate encounter with their dream girls, not some sort of group gang bang." He shrugs. "At least, not all of them. Okay, I take that back. Maybe that is the ultimate fantasy of some of them. But what they'll get instead is a one-on-one interrogation by an FBI agent."

Ryan nods. "Works for me. But the agents will still need reconnaissance to put the screws to our mystery men."

"That's where Donna comes in." Jack puts his hand on my shoulder. "As Sugar CEO's concierge, she'll greet each man personally. You know, take his coat, offer him a drink, give him the key to his room and walk him to the elevator, that sort of thing. It will also give her the face time that Arnie and Emma need to ID them. When she looks them in the eye, her lens feeds us video for an iris scan. Every time they open their mouths, we get a chance at voice recognition. Whenever they hit the elevator button or take her up on an offer for a libation, we have their fingerprints."

I smile at his brilliance. "So, where does this soirée take place?"

"It'll have to be a secluded venue, one away from any civilians," Ryan murmurs.

Arnie clicks away on his iPad. "Hey, I think I've got just the right place. There's a posh new hotel, practically next door to LAX. It's just passed the city inspection, furnishings are already being delivered, and the grand opening is still three weeks off."

"Great find, Arnie," Ryan says. Arnie gives him a silent nod, but his gaze falls on Emma to make sure she heard the boss man's kudos. Apparently not, since she's too busy combing through my pajama drawer. If Arnie doesn't make his move before this mission is over, he may lose Emma to his competition. I've got to give that boy another pep talk.

"Perfect! Acme will rent it out for an evening prior to the opening. The hotel's management will love making some pre-opening revenue. They will be told it's for a private corporate event, and that no onsite personnel will be needed because we'll be bringing in our own wait staff," Ryan says. "Sugar CEO will send a limo, courtesy of Abu. That way, there's no chance of them getting lost, and we can monitor any communication they have in transit."

"How will you break the news to the DOJ that I'm taking part in the mission?"

Ryan ponders that for a moment. "It was his grand scheme to use you as the canary in the Quorum mine shaft. If he wants to strike gold, it's time to move you to a different tunnel."

I'm almost afraid to ask, but someone has to say it. "How can we ensure the assassin won't get wind of this?"

"Our guess is that he's also tapped into the Sugar CEO database," Ryan explains. "If so, Arnie will have to create a sentry to block him from anything that signals future activity on their accounts."

"With Reynolds' watchdogs out front, won't I have to pass on all the fun?"

"If he thinks you're here, he won't be any wiser to your true whereabouts, Jack says. "Besides Emma's window dressing—or I should say, undressing—we'll transmit an audio feed from the house, so that he thinks he's hearing you talking to the children. Instead, it will be a recording."

For the first time in quite a while, Ryan graces us with a smile. "Should he show up at the hotel anyway, between the Feds and us he'll have quite a welcoming committee waiting for him."

And I'll finally be off the hook with the DOJ.

Just my luck he'll be here, watching Emma's strip tease.

I hope she does me justice.

CHAPTER 9

WHEN IT'S TIME TO MEET THE PARENTS

He has finally given in to your request to meet his parents. Whereas he's sullen and anxious, you're tickled pink, because it's proof that you've reached yet another major milestone in your relationship!

So that you're just as big a hit with them as you know they'll be with you, follow these very important courtesies:

Courtesy #1: Always come armed with a compliment! In fact, always come armed. A semi-automatic will do! With the right purse, it makes an elegant fashion statement.

Courtesy #2: No matter how thick it is, do not stare at his mother's mustache.

Courtesy #3: Should his father cop a feel, resist the urge to break his fingers. Remember, the bones of dirty old men over sixty are more brittle than the bones of your usual maulers, creeps under thirty.

Courtesy #4: Should his mother call you a "whore and a gold digger," pretend you didn't hear her. In fact, that is the ideal time to compliment her on her blouse, despite the fact that it is the size of a circus tent.

Courtesy #5: When your boyfriend asks, "So, what did you think of the old farts?" don't feel any compunction to tell the truth. Being polite is what real ladies do—

Especially ones who are whores and/or gold diggers, and can wait out the final days of two wealthy old farts. Remember, patience is a virtue!

The hotel where the operation is taking place is posh on the inside, gleaming on the outside. It juts eighteen stories above Pershing Avenue, in Playa Del Rey, right behind LAX. Its rooftop party deck is the perfect spot to enjoy a starlit sky.

What a great place to end the Quorum, once and for all.

My so-called concierge outfit is a vision in white, and in tight. It consists of a platinum blond Marilyn Monroe wig, tux tie, a breast-jutting bustier, a bum-hugging leather skirt, a tiny white bellman's cap, fishnet stockings, and high heels. I wear a beauty mark to the left of my lips.

None of this leaves room to hide a weapon, and yet I've never felt safer on a mission. Besides the FBI agents behind Doors One,

Two, Three, Four, Five, Six, Seven and Eight (each on a separate floor starting on the ninth, so that any shouting or crying can't be overheard) I'll also have Jack and Ryan out front and close at hand, just in case something goes wrong.

"Incoming," Abu murmurs into a mike that can be heard by everyone involved. "Sorry folks, his plane arrived earlier than expected."

The suspects are scheduled every fifteen minutes, beginning at eight o'clock. That gives Abu just enough time to drop off and turn back around for the next pick-up. Here's hoping most of these guys aren't as eager as this one, or our timing may be off. The last thing we need is for them to be bumping into each other in the lobby.

Sugar CEO Number 4 is tall and elegant. He wears a bowler, round spectacles, and a three-piece pinstriped suit. He carries a walking stick under his arm, and he bows slightly when he sees me. As his eyes sweep over me, his grin shows me he likes what he sees.

"Welcome. Your sugar baby is already waiting for you." My smile is accompanied with a broad wink. "Here is the key to your room. May I take your hat?"

The man hesitates for moment before nodding.

He won't need it where he's going. Gitmo is too hot for anything other than a sun hat.

His hand grazes mine as he hands it over. "Won't you be joining us?" His tone is hard, as opposed to hopeful.

In his dreams.

"Sorry, no. But trust me, you'll be captivated by all she has in store for you."

His eyes linger on mine for just a moment. Finally he sighs. "All the more reason to have you at my side, my dear. You know what they say: the more, the merrier."

"Perhaps next time," I say firmly.

The elevator rings its arrival. Saved by the bell. He pushes the button for the ninth floor, where his blind date awaits him.

When Sugar CEO Number 5 arrives, I'll send him to the eighth floor. The man who arrives after him will go to the seventh floor, and so on. By the eighth man, we'll be down to the second floor.

"Did you place him?" Arnie hears my question through my audio bug earring.

"Yeah, and I'm transmitting the intel to his FBI interrogator right now. He's a Swiss banker. Name is Dominic Gerstner."

I pray all the men aren't as creepy as this guy, but something tells me that I'll be in for a lot of this sort of King of the World attitude all evening.

I guess it comes with the territory.

We've now identified all Quorum members.

CEO Number 5, Guillermo Montezuma, one of Chavez's top toadies, was recently passed over as the next dictator of Venezuela. Montezuma's revenge is complete when he annihilates his political enemies, then turns Venezuela into an enemy with real teeth to its nemesis to the north: the United States.

Sugar CEO Number 6 is a Gunter Teichmüller, a German scientist renowned in the field of cyber warfare. Until now, we never knew his toys weren't just the domain of his government, but instead sold to the highest bidder.

Sugar CEO Number 7 is Konstantin Sherkov, a Russian venture capitalist whose wealth and power has the Kremlin worried. My guess is that his plan was to extend this pleasure trip into something permanent. If he plays ball, the DOJ can make that a reality.

The last Sugar CEO, Number 8, is Huang Zitong. He is a *shàngjiàng*, one of the highest ranking generals in China's People's Liberation Army. The scuttlebutt is that his ego-fueled bombast constantly puts him in hot water with his government's Paramount Leader. Apparently he sees the writing on the wall. Are China's bomb codes his chits in the Quorum's winner-take-all game?

"Hey, now that the last CEO just went up, why haven't we heard a peep from any of the FBI boys?" Jack murmurs in my earpiece. "At the very least, the top floor agent should have wrestled a confession by now."

To tell the truth, it seems weird to me, too. "Nope, strangely not a word from anyone. Should I go up and take a look around?"

"Yes, good idea. Now that Abu is back to stay, he can play doorman, so no one will be able to walk in by happenstance. I'll come inside to cover the lobby for you."

When he gets inside, I give him a kiss, then hit the elevator button for the ninth floor.

The elevator doors open with a whisper. I walk down the hall to the third room on the left, Sugar CEO 4's designated den of desire. The door is wide open.

Not good.

Neither is the fact that the FBI agent's throat is slit, and that he's bled out.

But where is Sugar CEO Number 4, Dominic Gerstner...?

Oh, shit! He's the assassin.

"Jack! Abu! Do you see what I'm seeing?" I shout.

"Donna? Donna, please repeat! You're breaking up!" Jack's voice sounds a million miles away. "And we've lost your video feed, too!...Hello, Donna?...Arnie, we need tech support here! Ryan, Donna's gone dark! We need reinforcements, now, on all the hotel exits! Abu, cover the front, in case the killer goes out that way, to make a break for it—"

In other words, I'm in this alone.

I don't wait for the elevator. Instead I take the fire exit. I'm seven steps to the floor below when, a moment later, Jack says, "Donna, the elevator isn't responding! We're going to try the stairwell."

The carnage on the eighth floor is in two places. Guillermo Montezuma bled out in front of the elevator. In the third room on the left, an FBI agent stares up at me with dead eyes.

I fly down the stairs to the next floor. Sugar CEO Number 6, Gunter Teichmüller, is laying in a puddle of his own blood. The agent in the room down the hall is gurgling his last breaths. I try to staunch the blood pouring out of him, but I'm too late. He dies in my arms.

I have the bright idea to skip down to the second floor. If the killer hasn't left the building, chances are he's there. If he hasn't made it down that far, maybe I can save two lives.

In any regard, my goal is that he doesn't leave here alive.

Dominic Gerstner is waiting for me.

I don't see him at first. Instead I see the body of another FBI agent, in the middle of the hallway. A knife sticks out of his gut, and he gurgles as he sucks in his last few breaths. His eyes beg me to help.

I crouch to my knees. Instinctively I reach for the assassin's knife in his gut. In one swift motion, I yank it out of him. I whisper that I'm sorry, that there is nothing more I can do for him.

At least now I have a weapon to fight his killer.

Out of the corner of my eye, I see a shadow, rising from somewhere behind me. By the time I feel his slight touch, the knife is already firmly in my grasp. I turn quickly, stabbing my attacker hard in the gut, not just once but three times.

I'm stabbing the corpse of General Huang Zitong.

Six feet away, Gerstner is laughing hysterically.

Not Gerstner, but Carl.

I see that now, when he peels off his face mask and pockets it.

Well, what do you know.

"So, it's Carl Stone who's taking down his Quorum buddies?" I shake my head in awe, even as I get into position to take him down. "Why, when you've sworn to protect them?"

"What can I say? I'm fickle I guess." Carl shrugs. "Like my wife."

He takes a stab at grabbing the knife, but I'm too quick for him. He nods, impressed.

"If you were going to kill them anyway, why didn't you just give us their names?" It takes a moment, but then it hits me. "Oh....wait, now I get it! You never knew their names in the first place." He dodges my elbow strike, but my high kick catches him dead center in the chest.

He grunts in pain, but shakes it off with a wag of his finger. "Yeah, turning on them would have been sweet. Too bad they were smart enough to stay anonymous, even to each other. But do thank the good folks at Acme for leading me to them, so I could thank each of them personally for their loyalty." He rolls his eyes. "Frankly, Dominic was the only one I had a bead on, so when he got the Sugar CEO invitation for a night of nookie with some dream bombshell, I thought, 'Hey, why not crash the party?' Have face mask, will travel, right?" He eyes me appraisingly. "You know, we still have time for a quickie. How 'bout it?"

I shake my head. "Sorry, you're no longer the flavor of the month."

The way his smile fades, I know I've hit a nerve. Well, too bad. I've moved on, and he should, too. "Seriously Carl, do you think you're going to get away this time? Acme and the FBI have this place surrounded."

He dodges my knife jab, then throws an elbow at my nose. As I duck, his funny bone finds the wall instead. To double his pain, I let loose with a sidekick. He grunts when my heel rams his stomach.

Carl gives me an admiring wave. "As much as you'd love me to stick around, doll, it just ain't going to happen." He glances at his watch. "In fact, my ride should be here, right about now."

"Liar!" I lunge at him, but he sidesteps my knife just in time. He grabs my arm and twists it behind my back until I groan in pain.

The knife clatters to the floor. He jerks me down on my knees. He's now within reaching distance of the knife.

As he reaches for it, my leg goes straight out. My heel finds his face, but not before he has a chance to grab the knife. Pulling my head back by my wig, he holds it at my throat. "Hey, I like you as a dumb blonde. Want to come along for the ride? Let me initiate you into the Mile High Club. "

"Really? You think you're going to just waltz out of here?"

"Let me prove it to you." He yanks me off my knees, and shoves me into the elevator. "Going up," he murmurs in my ear, then he licks it.

I slam my head into his nose. "You're a pig."

"Ouch!" Pained, he jerks back. To punish me, he slams my head into the elevator wall. "That's quite a term of endearment for your hubby."

"We're separated, remember? The papers are filed. It's only a matter of time, so grow up about it."

"*Boring*. Admit it, sweet pea, you miss Carl's love log. Hey, how about some elevator sex, to liven things up?" He kicks my feet apart and slams me up against the elevator wall, holding me against it with an elbow while he uses his other hand to pull up my skirt. A second later I feel his hand between my legs. A finger nudges aside my panties so that another can enter the sweet spot it seeks, moving in and out, faster and faster.

The elevator bell chimes. The door open.

"Ah, what a shame, we're already here! Time to get off." He lifts his hand so that we can both see his damp fingers. "But you've already done that, haven't you?"

I can make out the sound of the whirring of helicopter blades. Carl's right, his ride is already here. He drags me, kicking and screaming, toward it. It can't drown out the cacophony of police sirens, eighteen stories below us.

"So, what's the word, Donna, want to make a run for it with

me?"

"Go to hell!"

Instead, he crams his lips onto mine, prying my mouth open with his tongue.

Until I bite down hard on it.

"Damn it!" He shouts. His hand swings around to slap me, but he stops himself just in time. "Can't damage the merchandise. Or in this case, the fall girl."

He shoves me onto the deck and trots toward the copter.

I pull myself onto my feet. "What the hell do you mean by that?"

"You'll see," he shouts over the helicopter's revving engine. "Don't worry! You know what they say, orange is the new black!"

There is nothing I can do as his copter rises straight up into the night sky except shoot him a bird.

I circle back toward the elevator, but it's gone.

I'm running to the rooftop's stairwell door when it bursts open. Jack, Abu, and Ryan run through, along with a twenty-member FBI SWAT team.

Jack's eyes sweep over me with concern. When I look down at my white ensemble, I see why.

I'm covered with the blood of at least five men.

But I've got an alibi.

I think.

CHAPTER 10

IS HE LYING TO YOU?

Up until now, you've had no reason to think your new Mr. Maybe is anything but a gentleman and a scholar. However, there are a few red flags you should be aware of:

Red Flag #1: Your girlfriend claims he asked her for her phone number.

Wishful Thinking: He's planning a surprise party for you, and needs her help!

Reality Check: No, he's planning a date with her. And you'll be surprised how easy it is to break his neck when you find them kanoodling.

Red Flag Number 2: He insists you tell him your ATM number. Over the next couple of weeks, you notice your balance is dwindling down, in twenty dollar increments.

Wishful Thinking: Life is a Monopoly game. Eventually there will be a bank error in your favor.

Reality Check: Life is not a Monopoly game. It is a Survivor reality show. And right now, you are losing and he is winning. Time to exile him to the Island of Misfit Jerks. Otherwise, you're the loser.

Red Flag #3: He asks you for the keys to your new car because he says he wants to check the air in the tires. But three days later, you still haven't heard from him, let alone seen your car.

Wishful Thinking: He's taken your car to his mechanic for a thorough check-up, and it's taking longer than anticipated.

Reality Check: Face it, he's long gone. He's hit the road. He's outta there. Without you.

Perhaps things aren't really so bad. You may not have a cute ride, but all the walking you now must do is great for your legs.

"Mom, since it's Friday, can I sleep over at Babs' house? Wendy's parents have already said it's okay for her to go." Mary carefully keeps her head down as she pours syrup over her pancakes.

The reason she avoids looking me in the eye is because she's afraid I'll ask if Babs' mom will be in for the evening.

I won't ask, because I already know the answer: she won't, since she's a single mom who works as a nurse on the Hilldale Hospital night shift.

Three girls alone at a sleepover with Trevor and his buds, Wally and Eddie, on the prowl? I think not! Of course, if I accuse Mary of trying to pull the wool over my eyes, she'll pretend to be offended.

I'll just have to make this a win-win for both of us. She keeps her innocence, I keep my sanity. "Hey, why don't you host the sleepover instead? You can have a *Pretty Little Liars* marathon! I'll send Dad for pizza, and cupcakes from Beyond Heavenly. That way, Babs' mom doesn't have to rush home from work, should any emergencies arise. You know, like Wendy's and Wally's braces locking together when they make out."

Mary processes that for a moment. Having it over here may frustrate her boyfriend, but it allows her to save face with her girlfriends, and it certainly appeases me, now that she's figured out I know the score.

Finally she nods. "Alright, you've busted me. Does that mean we can't sleep in the media room?"

I smile sweetly. "Of course, honey, if that's what you'd prefer."

What I don't say, (and she doesn't know) is that all windows and doors are wired to infrared security cameras that trigger alarms, so there is no way the boys can sneak inside after Jack and I go to sleep.

Note to self: build a trap door on the threshold of the back entrance. Nothing deep enough to break a neck, but one that will do some damage to a teen boy's psyche.

Maybe fill it with water, then toss in a few baby alligators.

"If the girls want to have a few boys over, as long as we're home, too, I don't see any harm in it," Jack mutters from his computer, where he's writing up a report that he hopes will cover our asses after the bloodbath in Playa Del Rey.

Mary rewards him with a hug before running off to text her besties with the change of venue.

I pinch Jack's arm. "'No harm,' eh? Sure then, feel free to sit in on all the fun and games. In fact, maybe you can spin the bottle for them."

"That would be a lot more fun than watching you pace a trench in the floor."

"I'm worried. Why haven't we heard from Ryan?"

"He's probably getting reamed out, as we speak." He frowns. "My guess is that no news is good news."

"You'll be fine. I'll be Reynolds' scapegoat. Even if I'm not put permanently under lock and key, I'm sure to lose my job."

"Reynolds has nothing on you."

"Says who? Certainly not Carl. In fact, he boasted I'll be his 'fall girl.'"

"Sure, he talks a good game, but it won't be the first time you've managed to outsmart him. Speaking of games, isn't it time you gave Mary a little leeway? She's certainly not boy crazy."

"Not everyone can fend off peer pressure."

His right brow raises as he smiles. "Are you speaking from experience?"

"Of course not! I—I was as pure as driven snow."

"Are you telling me you never played Truth or Dare?"

"Never!" Yeah, sure, a few times. Not that he needs to know it. If we were playing now, I'd have to take the dare. And I'm sure I'd love it.

"How about Seven Minutes in Heaven?"

"Most of the boys I knew were too horny to last that long. Don't you mean seven seconds?"

"Aha! So you have played it." Jack leans over me. "Well, I've got staying power."

When his lips meet mine, his kiss, slow and long, promises to prove his claim.

Eventually I break away with a sigh. "You can prove it to me, tonight—after the boys leave, the girls are tucked in, and the alarm system is turned on."

"It's a date," he declares. "Speaking of which, rumor has it Emma consented to going out with Arnie tonight, especially when he scored tickets to the Growlers concert."

"Wow! Great move on his part."

"Yeah well, here's hoping he doesn't blow it during the meal."

"Why? Where is he taking her?"

"ZPizza. You know, the one with all the vegan choices. But he's worried he'll barf if she makes him eat the soy cheese."

"He is such a weenie. Every now and then it's good to get out of your comfort zone."

"You think so?" His strokes my cheek with his finger. "I now have a mission for your seven minutes of heaven: take you where no woman has gone before."

"That's quite a quest. But why put a time limit on it? Take a whole hour."

If where he's got his hand now is any indication, I'll never want him to stop. "In fact, take all night."

The phone rings. Reluctantly, Jack pulls away. The look on his face shifts from bliss to concern as he listens to whomever is on the other end. Then he says, "Yes, understood," and hangs up.

A wave of dread washes over me. "Who was that?"

"Ryan. Our client has ordered us to stand down."

"*What?*" I sit up straight. "What exactly does that mean?"

"The mission has been called off. Another contractor will finish the job." Slowly he turns and walks out of the room.

So, that's it? Acme will have nothing to do with hunting down Carl?

For the past few years, Jack has thought of nothing but my husband. Since he disappeared, Carl has been my obsession, too.

We are well aware we blew it this time. All the more reason to double our efforts in finding him, and bringing him to justice.

It's more than personal. It's self preservation.

The real hint that life is not a dream is when, at two in the morning, three FBI helicopters ready their spotlights on your house while some SWAT team leader yells your name through a bullhorn, followed by the words, "Donna Stone! We've got your house surrounded! Open the door, slowly, and come out with both hands over your head!"

Jeff and Trisha are standing at my bedroom door. When Jack jumps out of bed, they run into his arms. "Daddy, what's happening?" Trisha cries. "Why do they want Mommy?"

"It's all a big mistake. While she takes a second to get dressed, let's go outside and find out what this is all about." He hustles them out of the room with one hand, grabbing his cell phone off his bureau with the other.

Jack is calling Ryan to see why we've awakened in the third circle of Hell.

The loudmouth on the bullhorn warns me that all exits are covered, and that I've got less than thirty seconds to appear at the front door before they storm in, guns blazing, with orders to shoot to kill. I scramble for slippers and my official Acme ID card before flying down the stairs, counting down the seconds.

But the minute I hit the front stoop, I am cuffed, and my Miranda rights are shouted to me by the SWAT team's bootjacked flack-jacketed squad leader.

My perp walk is met by the slack-jawed stares of Jeff, Trisha, Mary and her sleepover friends, not to mention those of my now wide awake neighbors.

Penelope and her posse are among them.

This is how all of Hilldale learns that the woman married to the neighborhood DILF does not beckon him to bed in some lace teddy or a sheer baby doll peignoir, let alone a satin bustier and garter, but in his flannel pajama bottoms and a long-sleeved moth-eaten tee shirt touting the 1986 Metallica tour for *Master of the Puppets*.

Jack is talking to the SWAT team leader, but by the look on his face, I can tell he's not getting through to whatever lies within the stormtrooper helmet.

Just as my head is shoved down into the squad car, some brave soul yells out, "Right on! Thrash metal rocks!"

The agent driving the car looks back at me and frowns. I guess he thinks I'm some sort of political agitator.

I could explain to him I dig great guitar solos, but I don't think he'd believe me. In his eyes, I'm not normal. I'm not even human.

I'm a traitor to my country, just like Carl.

CHAPTER 11

YOUR MR. RIGHT: IS HE HOUSEBROKEN?

By now, he's always hanging at your place. And he's sleeping in your bed. He even borrows your toothbrush.

Yes, certainly you can get him his own toothbrush. Or you can allow him to park the one he already uses in your bathroom, along with his other toiletries.

You can also give him a drawer for his clothes, and point out that there are a few empty hangers in the closet for him.

If he's okay with all of this, maybe it's time to have the talk. You know the one: about moving in together.

This conversation has to be subtle, on so many levels. It is akin to bringing a pet into your home. In other words, you have to lay down some ground rules. Show him who's boss. Forget "If he were a tree, what kind of tree would he be?" The more important question is "If he were a pet, what kind of animal would he be?"

By recognizing these traits, you'll then know the best way to housebreak your new boyfriend:

He's a monkey if he: gives you backtalk and is stubborn.

To housebreak him, you must: practice rote commands, and reward him with little pieces of banana. Or sex. Something tells me he'll respond best to the sex.

He's a dog if he: pees everywhere but in the toilet bowl.

To housebreak him, you must: put him in a crate, with paper. Let him out only after he promises not to hit water, as opposed to porcelain.

Make sure he also promises to put the seat down.

He's a pig if he: eats in bed, farts in bed, and won't get out of bed.

To housebreak him, you must: put him in a crate and leave him there. Forever.

He's a cat if he: doesn't come home at night.

To housebreak him, you must: Neuter him. That's right, cut off his balls.

It's morning, in America.

At least, I think it's yet another morning.

And I pray I'm still on American soil. But any and all requests to see a lawyer are met with a blank stare or a guffaw, so I guess not.

It's hard to tell where I am, since there are no windows in my jail cell, and the glaring florescent lights over my head have been on since I got here, what, two, three days ago?

My interrogators come at me in around-the-clock shifts. I'm asked the same damn questions over and over again:

"How long have you been a Quorum double agent?"

"I have not, and never have been, affiliated with the Quorum," I declare firmly.

"Did you in any way know about, or participate, in the murder of the suspects and agents in the Quorum sting?"

"No, of course not."

"Where is Carl Stone?"

"I don't know," I insist.

"When did he last contact you?"

That one always makes me laugh. "What, you think he calls, or texts or something? He just shows up!" The fifteenth time I was asked this, I added, "Didn't they cover that in Terrorism 101, or did you skip class that day?"

My backtalk earned me four hours of head-banging rock and roll, played at ear-piercing decibles.

Had it been Metallica, I probably wouldn't be so grumpy now. I'm sorry, but Manowar just isn't in the same league.

Oh great, Reynolds is here. Carl may be the bane of my existence, but this jerk is certainly a close second.

He flops down in the chair on the opposite side of the table. After running through the playbook of his cohorts and hearing my stock answers to them, he hits the table with his fist. “Do you protect him because you still love him?”

At first, I’m too shocked to answer him. “He left me and our children. He allowed me to think he’d died. And whenever he reappears, my life goes to hell. If that’s your idea of marriage, I’m not surprised that you’re still single, Major Reynolds.”

Reynolds is towering over me now. Anger narrows his eyes into mean, gleaming slits. “Don’t you get it, Donna Stone? Game over! We’ve got what we need to put you away forever!”

“Oh yeah? What’s your evidence, exactly?”

“Maybe these will refresh your memory.” He tosses some photos onto the table. They fan out so that I don’t have to move them with my hands. Not that I could, since they’re cuffed to the arms of my chair.

The first picture shows me yanking the assassin’s knife out of the FBI agent posted on the second floor. Another shows me stabbing Huang Zitong, the Chinese general whom Carl shoved onto me. The photo is cropped in such a way that you don’t see Carl doing it, let alone that the man is already dead.

“This isn’t what you think! How did these conveniently come into your possession, anyway?”

“They’re digital stills taken from the hotel’s security webcam system."

"Then you should also have video footage of me manning the front desk between seven-thirty and nine-fifty that evening."

"Unfortunately, the feed was inconsistent. I guess the hotel hadn't tested it prior to Acme's rental, or they felt the price you paid for your party also bought you total discretion." He shrugs. "By the way, your prints are the only ones on the knife."

"That picture was taken as I was pulling the knife out, not sticking it in." Disgusted, I shake my head. "Don't you get it? Carl did this!"

"We have no proof that Carl was even there, let alone that he's stateside. We do have proof, however, that the banker who fled in the helicopter, Dominic Gerstner, put fifty million dollars in a Swiss bank account in your name. We also have proof that he secured a safety deposit box in your name, which holds fake IDs for you and your children, along with a letter from a private Swiss school, accepting your children for admission under their new identities."

"That's ridiculous! I'm one of the good guys. I would never run."

"I beg to differ, Mrs. Stone. Granted, I'm impressed with how cool you've played it. Every answer you've given each of our agents has been well-practiced." He shrugs. "But they've also been lies. When asked if you've ever been a Quorum double agent, you have emphatically denied any affiliation." He leans in. "Your role in the Gitmo break out will be your downfall, madam. From the beginning, the facts never added up. Despite your claim that you were drugged, none were found in your system. Two innocent men were murdered, including the plane's pilot. Not to mention Carl got away. Again, you were found with walk-away money and fake passports."

"Whether you believe me or not, I was set up."

"I don't believe you, Donna. And I can't believe you, because your actions speak louder than your words. Case in point: when Carl Stone first resurfaced in your life, you neglected to mention this to your superiors at Acme."

"Well...yes. I mean, technically. But at that point, no one had told me that Carl was a terrorist suspect."

His pause is accompanied with a smirk. "Is that why you passed him a detonator which could have set off the nanobomb at the World Little League game, costing tens of thousands of parents and children their lives?"

"Let's not forget I also got the detonator back from him, and shot him before he got away." My hands are shaking, I'm so angry. "I guess now you're going to blame his escape from the ambulance on me, too."

"I'm sure if I looked hard enough, I'd find a connection." He leans back. "If I remember correctly, you were arrested for killing Jonah Breck."

I nod. "Who turned out to be the titular head of the Quorum, remember?"

Reynolds shrugs. "At this point, I wouldn't doubt he was set up by you and your husband."

That has me snorting. "Again, for the record, *Carl and I are separated.* And speaking of Carl, thanks to Russian President Asimov's diplomatic strings, yes, the known terrorist in question was allowed back onto US soil, and within a hair's breadth of the president. Maybe that's something you should take up with your BFFs at the State Department."

"As we all now know, the assassination attempt on Asimov was merely a ploy: one that could have been suggested by Carl to the Russians, giving him the immunity he needed while getting close enough to assassinate the real target: the soon-to-be-appointed Russian ambassador, Jonah Breck." He smiles. "Having you there as back-up and an alibi was brilliant. Ryan Clancy's report on that particular mission states quite clearly that both you and your husband stayed in Breck's home, and that you had 'intimate relationships' with *both* men."

"If by 'intimate' you mean I played honeypot, I readily admit to doing so, in order to stop what we were told was to be an assassination attempt on President Asimov, as per the instructions of my employer, Acme Industries, and its client—who, by the way, also happens to be your boss, Mr. Reynolds."

"Acting as Breck's slut also gave you and Carl access to his computer."

Being handcuffed to my chair may be the only thing keeping me from grabbing the table and breaking it over Reynolds' head. If he comes close enough, I'll still be able to kick out his teeth.

"And both of you tracked him to his private island," he continues. "How do we know that killing him there wasn't a scheme hatched by you and your husband, to stop him from proving his innocence?"

"If that were the case, then why am I working so hard to take down Carl?"

"I'm not a marriage counselor, Mrs. Stone. But if you ask me, I'd say you have jealousy issues. Your husband runs off with Valentina Petrescu, so you get back at him by partnering, both professionally and intimately, with her ex-husband. At the same time, you pretend to do everything in your power to see that Carl hangs. And yet, you still love him."

"No I don't! I hate him."

"According to this, you don't." He tosses another file in front of me. Its caption reads

D. Stone - Sessions with Bob Hartley, MD, PsyD

"I can't believe you stole my file from my shrink!" I try to snatch it back, but Reynolds jerks it out of reach of my tethered hands.

He laughs. "Nothing is private when national security is at stake, let alone the heartsick ramblings of a jilted stay-at-home mom who fancies herself a player in the game of espionage. I guess that's why you jump into his arms whenever he's within reach."

"What? I hate it when he touches me!"

He stares at me in mock shock. Then slowly he pulls a folded note from his inside jacket pocket. "Really? You mean to say that you don't, and I quote, 'moan during our love play'? Or that your nipples don't, quote, harden at the sight of him? Tell me Mrs. Stone, are you damp right now, thinking about him?"

He's got Carl's letter. "You son of a bitch! Where the hell did you get that?"

Reynolds' lips are stretched wide in a victorious smile. "Your neighbor, Mrs. Bing, was kind enough to pass it forward. She presumed, rightly so, that anything showing your—how did she put it? Oh yes, 'depraved nature'—might shed some light on the charges against you. And by the way, she asked me to break the news to you that you've been kicked off the Hilldale Welcoming Committee. Apparently being greeted by a terrorist suspect sends the wrong kind of message about the 'hood, not to mention what it does for property values. Case in point: Abbottabad."

He turns to leave, still chuckling as he reads the letter.

He doesn't realize I've stood up behind him. And that I've flipped the chair over my head so that I can hold it, upside down, despite being chained to it.

I'm just about to bring it down over his head when I see Jack and Ryan, standing in the doorway. They stare at me, eyes open wide. Jack warns me with an adamant shake of his head.

Slowly I drop the chair back behind me as Ryan holds up a computer thumb drive. "Major Reynolds, we have some evidence that proves Mrs. Stone is telling the truth."

Disgusted, Reynolds' eyes roll skyward. "Bullshit! I've got an air-tight case against her."

"You're wrong," Ryan says firmly. "I'm sure you're aware that the footage you received wasn't complete. That's because these images were edited. In fact, we found a splinter feed across the street from the hotel, in an abandoned warehouse." He points to the pictures on the table in front of me. "Mrs. Stone's actions were altered *after* she encountered the dead men. For example, you'll notice the stills were cropped in such a way that you can't see everything going on in the hallway, which would certainly verify Mrs. Stone's contention that the real assassin was there, too." He points to the bottom of one photo, where the time stamp is visible. "Take note of the time, because it comes into play later."

"Give me a break," Reynolds mutters.

I'd like to break him, alright: across his skull, with this chair.

"On the other hand, Acme's feed, as seen through Mrs. Stone's contact lenses, show her downstairs from as early as seven-forty to nine-fifty," Jack explains. "After greeting the Quorum suspects and handing them the keys to the rooms where the FBI interrogators were stationed, she ushers them to the elevator. See for yourself."

He swipes the screen on his iPad. Instantly, a video showing the hotel's lobby appears on it. I sit at the front desk. A time stamp appears on the bottom left hand corner of the screen, showing that it is seven-forty, which was when Carl, disguised as Dominic Gerstner, comes through the front door. Granted, my demeanor changes slightly. It's obvious I'm uncomfortable in his presence, but at no time do I look as if I recognize him.

Each subsequent guest encounter is documented just as I remembered it. Reynolds can also hear Jack's, Abu's, Ryan's and my comments on what they witness through my eyes.

Reynolds shakes his head in disgust. "Even if this feed is legit and Carl was there, do you think I believe for a moment that she didn't know what kind of carnage was happening on the floors above that pretty little head of hers?"

Jack bristles. "I don't care what you believe. You say you want facts. Now you have them, even if you don't want to believe them. And they show she had no part in the killings, which is all that matters in a court of law."

"There is one fact against her," Reynolds retorts. "Donna Stone ushered those men to their deaths."

"No one expected Carl to be there," Ryan mutters.

"There's still no proof he was even there," Reynolds counters smugly.

"Maybe there is," I say. "Carl left his hat behind. I put it behind the concierge desk. Surely the FBI investigators took it, along with the rest of the evidence."

Reynolds nods grudgingly. "If so, we'll pull what we can from it." The faint buzz of his phone stops his train of thought. He taps it on. He's speaking too low for us to hear him, but the information he hears puts a frown on his face. "Dominc Gerstner's body was found, floating in a Marina del Rey harbor."

"Has the time of death been determined?" Ryan asks.

"It was found at six o'clock that evening."

"If that's the case, then he couldn't have been at the hotel," Jack points out. "Carl took his place."

Reynolds turns to me. “You’re free to go—for now. But at the very least, Acme ran a shoddy mission. The deaths of my agents prove it.”

I want to say the right thing, but really, what would that be? “I’m sorry” doesn’t begin to cover the shame and grief I feel over their loss, not to mention losing the one chance we had to take down the Quorum, once and for all.

CHAPTER 12

HOW TO DEAL WITH HIS OLD FLAME

Long ago, she broke his heart. He claims he's over her, but how can you be sure he's telling the truth? Here are some surefire signs she still lights his torch:

Sign #1: For some reason, he's forgotten to erase her telephone number from his cell phone. Worse yet, when you erase it, somehow it miraculously reappears.

Solution: Buy him a new cell phone, because this one is obviously broken.

Sign #2: When he goes out for a drive, his GPS tracker shows he's been by her place. When you confront him with this, he gets angry and insists you're crazy.

Solution: Replace the GPS tracker.

Sign #3: Sometimes he doesn't come home at night. When this happens, he claims he's having car trouble.

Solution: Buy him a new car.

Sign #4: His unconscious doodles look an awful lot like her name, with the word "Mrs." in front, and his surname behind it. When you point this out to him, he claims you're seeing things.

Solution: Buy new glasses.

Sign #5: When the two of you make love, the name he shouts out is hers. When you point this out to him, he breaks down and admits you're right.

Solution: Break boyfriend's hand. Specifically, the hand he uses to doodle.

Then give your next boyfriend the new cell phone, and the new car (equipped with a new GPS tracker).

Keep the new glasses. You look stunning in them.

"Are you sure you want another glass of that stuff? Aren't you on your third?" Jack puts down the pot he's washing in order to move the martini shaker just out of reach.

I snatch it back.

The next thing I know, Jack has slapped it out of my hand. He's sober, which gives him the advantage of dexterity. That, and he's not seeing double.

When I lunge for it again, he pours the perfect combination of good gin and olive-infused vermouth down the kitchen sink.

"Hey! That was the last of my Hendricks!"

"Good. Now you can sober up."

"What do you care? What does anyone care? How did Ryan so eloquently put it? Oh yes, now I remember! I'm on 'hiatus.'"

Which is another way of saying I've been terminated from the mission.

Jack nods toward the children, Emma and Arnie, all of whom have stopped eating their dessert in order to stare at us. Jack hisses, "He tried his damnedest to keep you in play."

"Bullshit. He sold me down the river." Nonchalantly I walk over to the wine rack. Jack is too busy stacking dishes to notice that I've palmed a seventy-dollar Booker Syrah and a wine opener. Who needs a glass? Besides, I've only got two hands.

As Jack tosses the pot into the sink, a green wave of Palmolive suds washes onto his jeans. "Damn it!"

Trisha's lip trembles. It's rare to see Jack lose his cool.

He waves at her. "Nothing to worry about, honey. Daddy just got a little wet. Hey, Mommy says it's fine if anyone wants a second helping of ice cream."

He tosses a new carton of Ben & Jerry's Chocolate Peppermint Crunch to Arnie, then follows it with the scooper.

While the kids are distracted by the thought of a mommy-approved sugar high, Jack continues, "Had Reynolds gotten his way, we would have lost five years of reconnaissance. Your termination on this mission was the only compromise he'd accept."

"In other words, Ryan didn't fight for me."

"Don't blame Ryan. Blame Carl. He's the one who set you up."

I shrug. Thank goodness Arnie found the splitter in the hotel's security feed."

"Wish I could take credit for that one but it was Jack's lead," Arnie says through a mouthful of ice cream. "Any more fudge sauce?" he and Jeff ask at the same time. Then they glare at each other.

Once again, they are rivals.

I sigh. "Arnie, don't you have a home?"

"Emma and I...I mean..." He looks over at Emma. They blush in unison.

"They're shacking up," Jeff mutters in disgust.

Suddenly I notice what Arnie is wearing: a *Star Wars* bathrobe over flannel pajama bottoms patterned in binary code.

Ha. I guess their little date went well after all. I hope he'll learn to like soy cheese.

Hmmmm. Wait a minute. "Arnie, what did you say? The lead on the splinter feed was Jack's?"

Arnie opens his mouth, but then his eyes shift to Jack and suddenly it shuts tight.

Now, that's a first.

Ah, I get it. *Valentina is back.*

Jack ducks just in time to miss the wine bottle, which crashes into the wall behind him.

He lifts his head, if only to raise a brow and nods in the direction of Mary, Jeff, and Trisha.

It's too late. They get the drift: Mommy is pissed off. She is also pissed.

My state of anxiety produces a psychic tsunami, knocking over everyone in its wake. Jeff, frightened, misses the Nerf ball he's been tossing at the wall in an attempt to best his record of eighteen one-handed catches. It ricochets off the ceiling before slamming into Trisha's Lego Princess castle.

As the pretty pink fortress explodes into eighty-eight separate pieces, Trisha bursts into tears and runs out of the room.

Mary glares at me. "Mom, get it together, okay? If not for yourself, then for the rest of us!"

She storms upstairs after her sister.

Emma and Arnie have already snuck away. I guess curt words and flying wine bottles don't fit into their fantasy of true love.

Mary is right. I am ashamed. If I'm going to have it out with Jack, I need to do it in the privacy of our bedroom. Or in a dark alley.

"When did your ex come crawling back out of the woodwork?"

Jack shakes his head as if he's got the headache from hell. "It wasn't her idea. It was mine. Donna, she's afraid for her life. She knows he wanted her dead for testifying against him. I had to convince her that helping us put him back in prison is the only guarantee she'll have for survival. "

So, Jack begged her to come back. Why am I not surprised?

"If she's so afraid of him, don't you even wonder how she got back into his good graces? She had to promise him something important." I'm baiting him to see if she told Jack that she's pregnant with Carl's child.

"I never question her methods. Just like I never question yours." Jack drops his head with a sigh. "But she delivered the goods. Besides the splitter feed, she gave us the name of his helicopter pilot. Reynolds already has him in custody. The intel the pilot gave us has put us back on Carl's trail." He frowns. "Don't worry, Valentina is back in hiding. She knows he's figured out she leaked something to us. I rue the day I introduced them. "

He still has feelings for her.

I should have realized Valentina will always be part of Jack's life, which means she is also a part of mine.

And since she's always playing both ends against the middle, Carl will be too.

Well, I'm going to nip that in the bud, once and for all.

Another woman might go into denial, pretend he's being honest when he tells her she shouldn't be threatened. Or she'd turn up the heat of passion so that he'd forget his old flame.

Not me. Instead, I tell him, "Sleep in the guest room tonight."

The sadness in his eyes makes me flinch, but I'm standing my ground. For now, its better this way.

If I'm sleeping in Jack's arms, I can't slip out and find Valentina.

When I find her, I'll find Carl.

There's a new canary in the mineshaft.

Chapter 13

Learning His Lingo

They say men are from Mars and women are from Venus, which is why we don't understand each other.

Pshaw! The key to unlocking his heart is learning to communicate with him. That said, learn these few key phrases of ManSpeak to prove you understand him completely:

Key Phrase #1: "Let's fuck." It's probably the most important phrase to know. Forget "Please," and even "Pretty please." He'll do anything you want and give you anything you want, if you say this to him instead.

Just make sure he gives you what you want before you go to bed.

Key Phrase #2: "Drop it, or you're a dead man." Whereas he responds to direct commands (such as "Drop it"), the operative word here is "dead." Feel free to use a visual, too. For example, a gun, cocked and aimed at his privates.

Key Phrase #3: "Money talks, or girlfriend walks." A man loves a woman who knows the value of a hard-earned dollar. So yeah, don't be afraid to limit your time, or to tie it to some specific monetary value. Say, a hundred an hour, cash on the nightstand.

Key Phrase #4: "Don't do that, or I swear, I'll bash in your head." Again, a direct command ("Don't do that") is preferable to something wishy-washy ("Um...no?" or "I wouldn't do that, if I were you"). Also, a threat works wonders, especially when accompanied by something that brings home the message. Like a bat aimed at his noggin.

When it comes to his spycraft, Arnie's lips are as tight as a gnat's ass. But they loosen up a bit when he's shoveling in a helping or two of my very berry pie.

It helps that the pie is laced with SP-117.

To make sure he'd be the pie's only victim, I left it out on the kitchen counter only a half-hour before his usual midnight chowboy run on my fridge. By the time he notices that I'm standing behind him, the pie has already lulled him into clueless affability.

"Oh, hi, Donna!" He spews fruit juice and golden brown crust as he giggles my name.

"Shhhh, Arnie. Let's not wake everyone in the house." I put a finger over my lips, then pour him some milk. Can't have him choking, now can we? At least, not until he gives me what I'm looking for. "Hey, I was wondering, where is Jack keeping Valentina?"

"Um....well, ya know, there are some things even Jack keeps from me. Unfortunately, that's one of them." He guzzles the milk, then gives a satisfying burp.

Lovely.

Manners aside, I force a smile onto my lips. But to make my point, I whisk away the pie tin out of reach. "So, you're telling me you have no idea where she is?"

Terror rises in his eyes. "I don't! I swear!" In desperation, he adds, "Hey, here's an idea: why not track Jack from the GPS coordinates coming from his cell phone?"

"You're brilliant, Arnie!" I grab Jack's phone from his coat and toss it at Arnie, along with my iPad. "Now, pull up his location from yesterday, say, around noon."

Any wariness he has in hacking Jack's cell dissipates in the heady aroma coming from the fresh baked cinnamon coffeecake I've pulled out of the oven. Arnie lunges at it, but I scoop it out of the way, just in time. "Bad boy! First things first."

Arnie gives a deep sigh and goes to work.

A few swipes later, I have what I need: an address in Manhattan Beach. I zoom in on a live webcam shot. It's a nice little cottage, on a quiet little street.

A part of me wants to play it straight; to just waltz up to the front door and ring the doorbell, but I know she's got a security camera trained to the front gate. If she sees me, she may panic and call Jack.

That's the last thing I'd want.

It's time she and I talked, just the two of us.

"Now, hack into the security system and read me the alarm code. While you're at it, put any webcam feeds on a loop."

Arnie nods. Every now and then his eyes shift longingly to the coffeecake, but he stays on task until he gives me what I want.

"Done," he declares.

"Good boy," I shove the cake his way.

The way he attacks it, you'd think this was his last meal on the way to the electric chair. While he eats, I murmur, "You won't remember we had this conversation, will you, Arnie?"

He shakes his head. I can barely make out what he's saying through lips laced in sugar and cinnamon, but it sounds like "Best. Babka. Ever."

The town of Manhattan Beach lies on a hill that slopes gently toward the ocean. Streets run parallel to the water, affording the majority of the homes on both sides of the road views to die for.

The cottage Valentina now calls home is about two blocks

from the beach and about six blocks north of the town's main boulevard. It is surrounded by high walls on all sides, and has a garage that opens onto an alley.

I catch my first glimpse of her when she goes out on the deck to watch a sherbet sun dissolve into the whipped cream haze that tops a dark water horizon. She doesn't betray her pregnancy by stroking her belly. It's only been a couple of weeks since I last saw her, and she's still as slim as ever.

Make that drawn and tired.

In the best of health, hiding from Carl is a draining experience.

Disarming the alarm takes a second. I'm in the house in no time flat. She is in the living room when I enter the kitchen from the garage. She's holding up something she's just taken out of a shopping bag from a baby boutique: Wonderland, in Los Angeles. It's an adorable little onesie, blue and white stripes.

She's hoping for a boy.

But of course. That would keep Carl on her good side.

"How did he take the news?" I ask.

She freezes then releases a bored sigh as she turns to face me. "For now, it's still our little secret, yours and mine."

I shake my head in disbelief. "Give me a break! After your testimony, carrying his child is the only thing standing between you and a bullet. We both know that."

She laughs, as if I've just told her the most delightful secret. "I have other powers of persuasion."

"What you really mean is that you sold out Acme, and will continue to do so, until Jack gets wise to you."

She shrugs. "You're stating a supposition. Give me the facts."

"Fact one: Acme plans a sting to round up the Quorum's hierarchy. Fact two: Carl kills one of the members, and shows up in his place. Fact three: the only way Carl would have known about the sting was if you relayed the message to him."

"Perhaps."

"But you had to do it in a way that didn't raise Jack's suspicions."

A smile creeps onto her lips. "You're getting warmer."

"In some manner, you made him an accomplice without his knowledge."

She laughs as if she hadn't a care in the world. "Ah, you see? You're better at this than you think! But I don't hear a question in all that blather."

"You planted a tracker on him when he wasn't looking, didn't you? That way, all Carl had to do was follow him."

Her eyes flutter, just for a moment.

The one valuable lesson I learned from my alcoholic father is that everyone has a tell. I've just found Valentina's. I brace myself for her lie.

"You know Jack better than that," she declares. "He's too smart for something that simple."

Yes, I know Jack. He wouldn't take something from a

compromised asset—unless he trusted her completely.

He trusts Valentina.

But Valentina sold him out. She got him to divulge the when and where and how of the Quorum-palooza.

And now she'll walk away, leaving others to clean up the blood-soaked mess.

If Jack knew this, would he forgive her?

No, of course not. She is his weakness. Carl knows it, and like he said, he exploits it every chance he gets.

I should kill her right now.

But I can't.

All I can do is pray that Jack believes me when I relay her confession. Even then, I'll have to find the tracker she somehow planted on him. That way, he'll have to face the truth that, once again, his Valentina sold him out.

But by then, Valentina will be long gone.

"I don't think there is anything we have left to say to each other. I did what I had to do, to survive. If and when Jack discovers the truth, he will accept it, even if you don't." She beckons me to the front door. "You're right about one thing. When I am far enough along, Carl, too, will have to accept my child, and me with it. Just as he accepts you." She smiles. "We both know it's the only reason he still hasn't killed you. Goodbye, Donna. Take good care of Jack."

Victory is hers, but it is as hollow as her future with Carl. She knows firsthand how hard it is to love a man who is beguiled by another woman.

I'm about to start for the door when we hear the faint buzz of a doorbell.

"UPS. Anyone home? We need a signature."

I'm just a few feet behind her when she opens it.

Her smile fades. Fear clouds her eyes.

Or is it resignation?

The bullet rips through her chest.

She stumbles backward then falls, face up.

The UPS man drops to the floor beside her, feeling for a pulse. When he looks up, he sees me staring at him.

I should have the advantage. I saw her assassin—Carl—before he saw me.

But I didn't move. I can't move.

Realizing that I'm still in shock, he smiles, stands up, and readies the gun again, this time for me.

"Sorry Donna, you know how it is: collateral damage. But don't worry, sweet pea! I'll make it look like one hell of a cat fight."

He expects me to tear up. Or to run for it. Or to stand my ground and reach for something, anything, that I can use as a weapon.

What he doesn't expect is the pity in my eyes. "Carl, you pathetic bastard! Valentina is carrying your baby."

I could not have hurt him any more than if I'd shot him through the heart.

His smirk fades even as his eyes grow wide. He falls to his knees.

Valentina's eyes, open and glassy, stare out at me over his bowed head. Her lips are moving, but her words are lost in the roar of his grief. As he curses and begs her to hang on, one of his hand cups her belly while the other tries to staunch the river of blood flowing out of her chest.

But it is too late. She is gone.

He staggers to his feet and looks around, taking in his surroundings for the very first time. Even in a safe house, the best spies know not to leave a trace of themselves. Valentina did an excellent job of adhering to this spycraft axiom, except for one thing: the shopping bag from the baby boutique.

Slowly, Carl picks it up. It takes a full minute before he can force himself to look inside. What he sees there causes him to breathe so heavily that I'm afraid he's having a heart attack.

When I take a step in his direction, he slings the bag at me, then doubles over and retches onto the wooden floor.

The blue and white onesie lands at my feet.

When finally he can breathe again, he forces his mouth into a smile. "Hey, how much do you want to bet that the kid wasn't mine? I mean, Jack's the one who has a thing for her. He's the one who loved her. Hell, I just used her."

I could kill him, right now.

But no, she's already done it. He's just a walking corpse. He won't admit it, but we both know it.

Good for her.

Without a backward glance, as if he doesn't have a care in the world, he strolls out of the house.

I call Jack and ask that he meet me here.

"So, Valentina was pregnant." Jack states this simply as a fact.

"Yes," I answer.

I've got to hand it to him. Unlike Carl, his reaction to the bloody corpse of the woman he once loved and married was composed.

Only one fallen tear gave him away.

I got an hour's head start before he called the Acme clean-up crew.

When he came home, we pretended life in the Stone household was business as usual. We orbited the children, asking them questions about their day, their homework, and their friends. Did they notice Jack's frosty politeness to me, or that I seemed a bit distracted?

Now that they are in their beds and we are alone together in ours, I expect him to insist I feel his pain.

He doesn't disappoint. "You knew of her pregnancy, and you

went ahead and killed her, didn't you?" There is no doubt in his voice, only repugnance.

I can't believe my ears. "You think I could have done that...to her, while she was in that condition?"

"You hated her, so yes. Tell me the truth, was it because you thought it was my child?" The ice in his stare causes me to flinch. It hurts more than any slap or punch.

"How dare you! I've already told you! It wasn't me, it was Carl!"

He doesn't say a word. He won't even look at me.

I can't believe he thinks I'm lying to him.

Saddened, I shake my head. "Carl was right."

He turns to me. "What's that supposed to mean?"

"He knew she was your weak spot, and that's why, once again, he was able to pull the wool over your eyes."

Jack's laugh is brittle. "You don't know what you're saying."

"You may not want to hear this, but I'm telling you anyway, Jack Craig." I move to his side, but Valentina's ghost still stands between us.

What can she say to him now? Nothing. It's time he listened to me. "Carl won because he knew how badly you wanted to believe she cared for you. He won because you cared more about protecting her than about finding him."

The thought that Jack would think I'm lying to him makes me angry enough to say something I'm sure I'll regret, but I can't help myself. “Was he right? Was the baby yours?”

In a flash Jack’s fist heads my way, stopping just an inch short of my nose. Like everything else that hangs between us, our mutual pain stops momentum in any direction.

Carl knew he lost me to Jack.

But when Jack lost Valentina, I lost Jack.

So I guess I lost to Carl, too.

I head toward the door. Jack doesn’t stop me.

Once again, we’ll sleep in separate rooms.

In the middle of the night, as Jack snores away gently in the guest room, I take his cell phone from the bureau.

Then I go down to the kitchen, where Arnie munches away on cold fried chicken.

I don’t have to drug him. Instead I beg him for one more favor: to scan Jack’s phone for any received texts containing a tracker that would have given Carl his location at any time.

In less an hour, Arnie finds what I suspect. It is embedded in a text message that reads, simply:

Thank you for caring, always, –V

I will take no joy in showing it to him.

It may prove I’m right, but then so is Valentina. He will

forgive her because he respected her instincts for survival.

It is a mother's instinct. We may sacrifice ourselves for the greater good, but when it comes to our children, we will protect them at any cost.

Even if the cost is the lives of others.

CHAPTER 14

HOW TO READ HIS MOODS

The worst thing that can happen in your brand new relationship is that you misinterpret his moods. Here are four examples you should take to heart:

1: He is sullen. This indicates that he needs some "alone time," so forego any urge to (a) be next to him every minute of every day; or (b) follow him into the bathroom; or (c) shadow his every step, hiding behind corners whenever he turns around.

2: He doesn't acknowledge you when you talk to him. Again, he needs some alone time. Do him a favor and talk to your friends instead. Or a close family member. Or your shrink, especially if you're having visions of beating him black and blue, just to hear him say "Stop! Please!"

3: He doesn't answer your calls to his cell phone. This is yet another indication that he needs some alone time.

That said, do not (a) presume his phone is broken, and buy him the latest iPhone; or (b) trade in his brand new iPhone for an Android-equipped Smart Phone; or (c) lock him in your spare bedroom, so that you don't need to call him in the first place.

4: He takes off, without giving a forwarding address. I'll bet you can guess the cause of this action. Yep, he needs alone time.

Sadly, granting it will leave you in a quandary. How can you live without him? More to the point, how dare he try to live without you?

The solution: plant a GPS chip in his arm and voila! You'll finally know where he is at all times!

On Saturday mornings, the husbands of Hilldale do their yard work.

I've come to the realization that I can gauge the status of my neighbors' sex lives by how early their lawns are sheared and their hedges are trimmed. Those men whose sleepy wives fend them off by claiming to be too tired for sex find the morning frost easier to face than a frigid dismissal of their amorous advances. On every block in our town, the buzz of at least one rider mower can be heard as early as seven o'clock.

This morning, Jack was out of the house, and on our mower by six.

We aren't exactly sleeping well these days, let alone sleeping together.

I take out my frustration on my bedroom windows. But no amount of Windex with Ammonia D and elbow grease will take away the pain of his distrust.

Yes, had Valentina hurt him or my children, I would have been the first one to cut her throat. But I didn't do the hit. Jack should know I could never kill a pregnant woman.

Even one whom I suspect is Jack's true love.

I'm on the fifth pane of the second window when I see a man approaching our house. He has a grizzled beard that reaches almost to the waist of his flowing black cassock. At his neck is the white collar of a priest. I recognize his hat as a skufia, like those worn by Eastern Orthodox clergy.

At first he hesitates when he sees Jack coming toward him on the rider mower. But then he straightens up and marches forward, a man on a mission. My killer instincts steel me for the worst. Should I run to my vanity table, where a gun is hidden in the false bottom of a drawer? And if so, can I make it back to the window in time to protect Jack?

As it turns out, Jack also sees the man. He too is wary of him. He stops the mower, but doesn't turn it off. The sound will muffle a gunshot, should one go off. Whereas his left hand stays on the steering wheel, his right arm goes limp at his side. If necessary, it will reach down by his ankle to grab the gun strapped under his track pants.

They talk for a moment. I can't hear what is being said over the hum of the mower, but the power of the man's words can be seen on Jack's face. I can't even imagine what he might say that could sharpen Jack's studied passivity into wariness, then cleave it with despair.

Finally, the priest hands Jack an envelope and walks away.

Each second seems an eternity when the man you love is in pain. It takes him a moment to rip open the envelope, and just two minutes to read its one-page contents. The mower is turned off as he contemplates its message. For the next six minutes, while he sits there staring straight ahead, the chirping of birds is all that can be heard.

No sound is more deafening than grief.

At long last, Jack leaves the mower and makes his way into the house. When he sees me at the top of the stairway, he doesn't say a word. He doesn't have to. I read the anguish in his eyes.

When I get downstairs, I find him in the kitchen. He takes my hand and pulls me into the living room with him, but waits until we're both sitting side-by-side on the couch to hand me the envelope.

When I open it, a key falls out into my palm.

My hands shake as I take the letter and read it:

My dearest Jack,

If you are reading this, it is because I no longer walk the earth. Maybe that is for the best, since, if I am to be honest with myself, I quit existing long ago.

Even before I left you for Carl.

In truth, I was dead to this world before we met.

You did your best to keep me from being a living ghost. I betrayed you, and yet you still believed in me.

But my dear sweet Jack, I had made a pact with the devil. He owned my soul.

What you did not want to believe was that, eventually, he would come to collect it, no matter your attempts to redeem me.

If you are now reading this, know that Carl succeeded in doing so.

With my help, he found the Quorum through you.

God knows I didn't want to do it, but I felt it was necessary, for me and my child. Please find it in your heart to forgive me.

Carl is devious enough to do his best to make any evidence of my death point to either you, or to Donna. Just as, should either of you had fallen prior to my own death, he would have done his best to make me out to be the perpetrator.

I gladly played the pawn in his attempts to fester the doubts that plague you both. I reveled in the knowledge that you might still love me, despite my deceptions. Only from beyond the grave can I summon the courage to tell you the truth:

I could never love you with the passion with which you loved me.

For me, passion is dark and illicit. It is a cruel master who takes everything and regrets nothing.

It was inevitable that Carl was my passion.

Please forgive me, Jack. I know the truth hurts. Now that I am free from the pain of my desire, I can set you free, too.

If you have not yet deduced Carl's plan, it is to remake the Quorum with investors of his own choosing.

To impress them, he has planned an extravagant exhibition of terror. You already know it is to take place on Donna's birthday. I leave you with this key, which you know well. It leads you to the one last bit of intelligence you seek: where to find the devil who has plagued us all, before he completes his mission for world annihilation.

It is my very late attempt at redemption, dear Jack.

I wish I had more to give you. In truth, I wish I could give you back all the love wasted on me. I was never worthy of it, whereas she has more than proven that she is the one you were meant to love.

Don't waste a lifetime figuring this out. My final prayer is that, unlike me, you'll have nothing to regret.

Valentina

So, there will be a new Quorum. One molded by Carl. One rebuilt in his image.

Talk about trading one hell for another.

Jack waits until I drop the letter in my lap before reaching for my hand. He doesn't speak until the last of my tears has fallen. "Donna, she's wrong about two things." He looks me right in the eye. "I figured out a long time ago that she never loved me. But I was worried that you would never believe me if I told you I had accepted this and had moved on."

"You're right. I thought you hadn't gotten over her. I guess that's why I asked you if the child she was carrying was yours." I sigh. "I'm glad you didn't hit me. At the same time, you had every right to be angry. Once again I doubted you."

"That's only because Carl is a master at head games. For once, though, Valentina outplayed him." He pats my hand. "Donna, I also know you chose me over Carl, even before you thought he had killed me."

"Jack, when I thought I'd lost you... and then you came back to me... all I could think of is how you'd say goodbye again if she wanted to come back to you..." Can he make out my words through my sobs?

"Donna, I swear to you! I would have told her what I'm telling you now: that yes, I had loved her once, a lifetime ago. And yes, I grieved her loss for a very long time." He pauses. "But I would have told her I'd finally found the love of my life. That I'd found my family."

Now I'm bawling like a baby.

He's crying, too. Or maybe he's laughing. I can't tell, because his face is blurred by my tears, which just won't stop.

"Donna, when I met you, I saw my pain mirrored in everything you did, and said. In how you channeled your grief in our profession. And how you protected your precious family. I wanted to protect you. I...I fell in love with you." He stops to clear his throat. "But I had to wait until you no longer doubted my feelings for you. Until you realized that I love you. Always and forever."

My kiss takes him by surprise. Why is that? Can't he guess I've waited much too long to hear him say this?

Valentina was a fool to love Carl. I was that foolish, too, once long ago.

Jack forgave us both.

Without forgiveness, there is no love.

Finally, our lips part. My hand reaches for his and the key falls into my lap.

Can it save all of us from Carl?

I hold it up. "This is too small for a door lock, but too large for a safety deposit box. Do you know what it opens?"

"Yes. A very special keepsake box that once belonged to Valentina's father." He pulls me into his arms. "And I also know where I'll find it. Time to pack up again."

"Where to, this time?"

"Paris," he says sadly. "While we're there, we'll lay her to rest there."

I lean back onto him. Through his tee-shirt I can feel his heart pounding steadily, like a metronome meting out all the reasons why he will always be worthy of my love.

Trust. Devotion. Passion. Honor. Courage.

His heartbeat also reminds me that if we're to stop Carl, time is of the essence.

My birthday is less than a week away.

CHAPTER 15

PLANNING YOUR FIRST WEEKEND GETAWAY

Squeeeee! He wants to take you away for the weekend!

So that this is the first of many fantasy getaways with the new man in your life, take these items with you. They'll ensure you take off as much as you carry on:

Item #1: A bathing suit. Stay away from the one your mother bought you. Instead take something with tiny straps that break easily, especially when you're being hit by a ten-foot wave. Nothing says "I'm available" like a naked woman on the beach!

Item #2: A sun hat. The bigger, the better. However, to avoid helmet hair, don't wear a hat that is (a) wool, (b) leather, (c) baseball (d) a helmet, or (e) ten gallon.

Item #3: A paddle. Yes, you can use it to play Ping-Pong in the hotel's rumpus room. But it is more than likely he'll be using it on your sunburned rump, after you've expressed your fantasy to "be his little girl." Be careful what you ask for!

Item #4: A taser gun! Consider this an emergency only item. For example, you can use it in case he (a) books you in a roach-infested hellhole inhabited by a lot of lowlifes, (b) makes you carry both his bag and yours, up several flights of stairs, or (c) he somehow forgets your safety word. With one shock, he's sure to remember it the next time.

The flight to Charles De Gaulle puts us in Paris just after dusk. It takes an hour by car to get into the city proper. Billowing blankets of rain, caught in the streetlamps, shimmer around us in a blustery wind.

Our first stop is the Cimetiere du Pere-Lachaise, where we will bury Valentina.

She'll be in good company. Besides Jim Morrison, Oscar Wilde, Edith Piaf, Chopin and Gertrude Stein, Valentina's father was also laid to rest in one of the graves among Pere-Lachaise's tree-lined cobblestoned streets of the dead. He was a Romanian professor whose anti-government discourses made him an enemy of the state and put him in a notorious hard labor camp.

It also put Valentina, a teen gymnast at the time, on the path to espionage. She was a reluctant spy for the SIE—Romania's Foreign Intelligence—before Jack turned her into an Acme asset.

When her cover was blown, he married her to give her diplomatic immunity.

Along the way, he fell in love with her.

We arrive right at dusk. I stand beside him as her coffin is lowered into a freshly dug hole in the center of this one-hundred-and-ten-acre garden of stone angels. Like Jack's, their anguish is etched in every pore of their faces.

He crouches down and scoops up a handful of the freshly churned dirt, only to let it filter through his fingers. Each clod and pebble hits her coffin, a timpani of regrets.

When she was alive, I could not stop him from having feelings for her.

Now that she is dead, I cannot stop him from mourning for her.

To love him, I must accept this.

As we walk away, we pass a man in a wheelchair. He wends his way carefully down the old cobblestone paths, steering clear of the gnarled roots of the oak trees that shade this sad city of the dead.

In the mere second his eyes meet mine, I am touched by the sadness I see there.

I know in my heart that my own reflect something very different: the hope that Jack can now love me fully, and with an open heart.

We reach Avenue de New York in time to see the light show

on the Eiffel Tower, which splashes and sparks to the delight of the crowds at its base.

If only Jack and I could be among them, enjoying the sights and sounds of the most famous city of love.

Despite our dire circumstances, Jack is actually smiling. "I know a little place we can grab a quick bite to eat. It's right around the corner from my old place."

He takes me into the neighborhood known as Le Marais. The bistro is in a narrow alley. Inside, it is packed with locals. As we wait for our fish entrees to arrive, the hum of lively conversation hits us on all sides. Anyone watching us would think he only has eyes for me, but I know better. Like any good spy, his ears are perked and his eyes are focused on the hubbub around us. Before Acme assigned him the role of my husband in order to smoke out the real Carl Stone, he was running Acme's European operations.

A blithe conversation between the svelte, fashionably attired middle-aged couple at the next table puts a smile on his lips. He nods in the woman's direction. "Her lover just walked in. Her husband insists she invite him over."

Now I am laughing, too. "You miss it here, don't you?"

He shrugs. "Maybe someday, when the children are older, we'll have an opportunity to spend more time here."

"That would be interesting." I mean that on many levels. I wonder if he means we should request a joint transfer. Or does he plan on us resigning from Acme?

But that's the problem: assassins don't retire. We'll always be looking over our shoulder, if not for Carl and the Quorum, then for the next Carl, and the next Quorum.

Sadly, Paris is not the sort of place one can hide in plain sight.

And then there is the issue of his past with Valentina. Even if she wasn't buried here, Jack is more likely to feel her presence in this town, where he loved her so passionately, and where she left him so callously.

At this point in our relationship, Jack knows me well enough to guess my thoughts. "I'd go to the end of the earth with you, Donna, you know that. As far as I'm concerned, it doesn't matter where we are, as long as we're together. Forever."

This is my wish, too.

Unfortunately, so would Carl, I think. That's why we have to put him away, once and for all.

When our meal comes, we eat in silence.

As we get up to leave, I notice that the woman and her lover hold hands under the table while her husband rubs her neck. When the husband gives me a wink, the wife frowns petulantly.

Passion is simple, whereas love is complicated.

I am happy to get out of there. Now that the rain has stopped, the air smells fresh and clean and new.

Jack and I have a chance at a new beginning.

I won't let Carl ruin it for us.

"We're here," Jack says.

I look around us. We're now about three miles down and across the river from the Musée d'Orsay, driving onto a stone bridge called Pont Marie. It takes us onto a small island known as Ile St. Louis, which sits in the middle of the river. On the far side of the island is Notre Dame.

Jack drives around the island until we are facing the Seine's left bank. Finally he pulls into a narrow alley and turns off the engine. "We're here." He points up to a top floor window in one of the many centuries-old buildings which jut out over the river.

"Is it some sort of safe house?"

"No. It's the home of a dear friend." His smile fades. "The man who lives there, Anton Gregorescu, was a friend of Valentina's. He brought home three medals for the Romanian Men's gymnastics team. He was very much in love with her."

"Did he defect with her?"

"If he had, he wouldn't be a paraplegic today. Without his help, she couldn't have escaped. He covered for her. Anton paid dearly for his lies. To make an example of him, his spinal cord was severed, and he was institutionalized."

"That's horrible!"

"Yes, it was. Thank god Ryan was successful in negotiating his release." Jack takes a flashlight out of the glove compartment, points it to the top window and flicks it on and off: fast three times, slow twice, then fast twice once more.

A moment later, we spot a candle's glow in the window.

Jack nudges me. "Time to go. And by the way, he took the news of Valentina's death very hard."

As hard as Jack took the same news, I wonder? If so, she certainly cast a spell on the men in her lives.

On everyone but Carl, that is.

The sixth and highest floor of 38 1/2 Quai d'Orleans is reached by a narrow, rickety staircase. By the time we reach Anton Gregorescu's door, we are both out of breath.

I can see why Jack felt the need to warn me about our host. His red-rimmed eyes and grimace are signs of a man in mourning.

He is the paraplegic we saw earlier this evening, in the cemetery.

I shake his hand when Jack introduces us. Jack bends down to give Anton a hug. They have a quick exchange in French, then Anton hands Jack a small metal box. When Anton asks him something about Valentina, Jack frowns, and his eyes find mine.

Anton follows his gaze. He pauses then asks in English, "Did she die quickly?"

Without hesitation, I lie and nod. He knows otherwise. The tears well up in his eyes and fall into his lap. And yet, I don't get the feeling that Anton is a helpless man.

Despite the fact that his legs are as thin and lifeless as a marionette's, Anton has large biceps, and his shoulders and chest are massive. His walls are lined with photos that show him at the peak of his vigor, brimming with youth and promise, floating in perfect formation over the parallel bars.

I've no doubt he is still a brute of a man.

Another wall is a shrine devoted to Valentina: as a child, performing somersaults with other tots her age. As a pre-teen, her arms raised in triumph as she accepts a medal. As a young woman, in jeans and a man's pea coat, mugging for the camera.

There is another picture, too. In it, she stands beside Jack on the steps of a Paris courthouse in a simple white shift, and a bouquet in hand.

Anton isn't there. I presume he was in some Romanian hellhole of a jail.

"We all do what we must," he says, as if reading my mind. "I have never regretted the path that got me here." His hand swings to the double French doors. Directly beneath them is the Seine. Across the river is Notre Dame. Beyond it is a breathtaking view of the western half of the city, all the way to the Jardin du Luxembourg. "I live in the very heart of Paris, and I am free. The cafes, the restaurants, the Jardin des Tuileries. What more can one ask for?"

I let loose with a chuckle. "How about an elevator?"

He laughs, too. "Ah! But you see? I have one!"

He rolls himself over to a low cupboard on a far wall. When he opens it, I see what he means: inside is a dumb waiter large enough to hold a wheelchair. "Up until this week, my home has been my fortress."

Jack raises his head from the task at hand, memorizing a tiny sheet of paper in the box. "Why is that?"

"In a day or two, I will have yet another visitor." His smile holds only sadness. "He too will be given a box. It is somewhat bigger than your own. I have no idea of its contents, only that Valentina presumed it would buy you the time needed to complete your mission."

He stops at the sound of creaking steps, coming from the stairwell outside the apartment. Anton shoves his wheelchair to a desk, where a computer sits. A tap of the keyboard brings a webcam visual onto the screen. Two men dressed in black can be seen, inching their way up the stairs. They are already on the third landing.

"Alas, the guests I dread have arrived early. It would be wise that you leave before they reach my door." He points to the dumbwaiter. "It will be a tight squeeze for both of you, but you'll find it a very quick exit."

I shake my head. "We can't just leave you here!"

"But I insist. I owe my life to Valentina. If it is time to pay that debt, then so be it." He lifts his head defiantly. "Don't worry about me. Once they get what Valentina promised them, they'll see no need to hurt the poor cripple."

Jack pulls me with him toward the dumbwaiter. We have to crouch down to enter. By pulling a small lever, we begin our descent.

The dumbwaiter lets us out into the alleyway where we've parked the car.

We've just hopped in when Anton's windows open. The next thing we see is his wheelchair being rolled out and over the side, by one of the men.

He falls with a splash into the Seine.

Jack is about to leap out of the car when suddenly we hear a blast. Anton's apartment is a smoky fireball.

"Their box! It held a bomb!"

"That's my girl." I can't begrudge Jack his pride in Valentina. "Maybe it's for the best that Anton was pushed."

I shake my head. "God rest his soul."

Jack laughs. "I doubt that will be the case."

"Why do you say that?"

"Not only was he a gymnast, he's an expert swimmer, too. For that he doesn't need his legs."

"You're kidding, right?"

"Not at all. How do you think he built back his upper body?" Jack starts the car. "So tell me, how do you feel about Mexico?"

CHAPTER 16

FLIRTING.... WITH DISASTER

There's certainly nothing wrong with flirting to grab a guy's attention. However, when doing so, keep in mind that men read signals differently than women. Here are six moves he'll never misinterpret:

1: A wink. He'll find it sexy! (But just once. Otherwise he'll think you have something in your eye, in which case he'll think you'll need a trip to the emergency room, and run in the other direction.)

2: Tossing your hair to one side. The hair toss is the international signal that you want his attention. (However, forego the head scratch, which indicates crabs, lice, or other parasites.)

3: A tee shirt that says, "Hey, you! I'm available!" Putting something in writing—especially breast-high–is the best way to get his attention, and he'll love the fact that you tell it like it is. (In fact, forego the tee shirt altogether. Go ahead and get this message tattooed on your chest.)

4: Hone a great pick up line. Nothing along the lines of "You don't smell as bad as most guys your size" or "Watching you eat makes me want to barf." Instead, make it positive and complimentary.

5: A kiss. What a great way to greet a handsome stranger! Nothing is more inviting that an open mouth. (Word of caution: be sure to get off your knees. Otherwise you'll give him the wrong first impression.)

6: A low-cut blouse, paired with a micro-mini skirt and five-inch heels. Better yet, forget the blouse and the skirt. The heels by themselves say, "I'm available, and I'm all yours...and his....oh yeah, and I'm up for that dude over there, too."

You've been dating Mr. Maybe long enough that passionate desires are erupting in both of you. (Granted, his are more obvious, since he has an outie, and it has a mind of its own.)

Isla María Madre rises higher and steeper from the turquoise Pacific Ocean than her sister islands, María Magdalena and María Cleofas.

Am I the only one who finds irony in the fact that Mexico's notorious prison was built on an archipelago named after the three saintly women who attended the Resurrection?

That's okay. My mission is a resurrection, too, of sorts:

When I leave, I'm taking the prison's biggest bad-ass with me.

That would be Hector Negrón de la Moraga.

This Forbes 100 billionaire's cash flows in from the tons of methamphetamine he smuggles stateside. His drug mules are many of the American socialite junkies who hang at his Cabo San Lucas nightclubs and resorts.

But because the gangbangers known as *Los Corazónes Rojo*s are jonesing to take over his territory and have put a price on his head, the first six months of his prison sentence have been spent in solitary confinement.

No wonder he felt it was time to cut a deal with the United States. Spill his guts, as it were. Before they are spilled for him, all over the prison yard.

He got the Feds' attention by explaining that he launders his dirty drug money through a blind corporation: a real estate company which builds Mexico's many gated communities and private stucco palaces.

Not only does he know where his rivals live, he's also got the floor plans of all their estates.

Including the security codes.

If the note Valentina left in her father's tin box is correct, he built the brand spanking new villa the Quorum uses as the south-of-the-border headquarters. This is where we'll find Carl and his new friends.

We must find them by tonight, if we're going to stop them, once and for all.

Happy birthday to me.

The United States, Great Britain, France, Germany and Japan want to put the Quorum out of business, once and for all. But some crooked Mexican politicos have halted Hector's extradition. Their allegiance is with *Los Corazónes Rojos*, which has a hit out on him.

That's where I come in. I'm breaking him out of this hoosegow. In return, he's going to point out the Quorum's safe house, and provide us with its floor plan and security system data. Afterward, the Feds will let him live stateside, where he'll be put in the Federal Witness Protection Program.

Hector's financial portfolio may be humongous, but his physique is petite, which is why his nickname is El Chihuahua. Here's hoping he lives down to it, since smuggling him off the island won't be easy under any circumstances.

Now that the prison is within sight, the tug's low, sad bellow puts all hands on deck. The Mexican flag flaps loudly on the stern pole. I presume no masts are half-raised inside the prison, either.

Certainly not El Chihuahua's, now that his paid-by-the-hour *puta* is here.

That would be me.

The other women standing with me on the tugboat's deck—all wives, girlfriends and whores on their way to their monthly conjugal visits with the murderers, thieves, and drug dealers who live within the prison's walls—adjust their lips upward into smiles, while tugging the necklines of their too-snug blouses even lower.

In lockup, orifices may be readily available, but bountiful cleavage is not.

My breasts are already propelled high, front and center. My skirt is short and tight, whereas my high heels are long, pointy and packed for a punch: one is tipped with a knockout drug, the other with a serrated blade.

So yeah, I guess I'm ready, too.

There are at least forty guards on the grounds, and another six in the turrets of the towers topping this castle-like compound. Their whistles and catcalls can be heard loud and clear as we women maneuver our way up the chipped stone steps leading to the prison's two-story solid steel gates.

Being manhandled (ostensibly for hidden weapons or breakout tools) has many of the ladies wincing. But those who, like me, are looking for an extra half-hour with their menfolk smile and purr a few promises they hope will be forgotten when it's time to leave this hellhole.

The metal detector beeps when I saunter through. The guard on duty smells as if he's taken a hit off every bottle of tequila that's been smuggled in today. He presumes it is the thick-ribbed bracelet on my arm that set it off. All the same, he fondles my breasts between his rough palms, as if they're a pair of ripe melons.

Tit for tit, I pinch his breast harder than he tweaked mine.

"*Usted me está haciendo caer en amor con usted,*" he says, with a smirk.

Why am I not surprised that he actually likes a little rough play?

"What a douche," Jack mutters into my tiny diamond stud earpiece. Obviously, he doesn't like what he sees. No boyfriend would, right? "Seriously, Donna, you have my permission to kill him, now, if you want." By his tone, I know Jack means it.

"*Mas tarde, mi amo*r," I murmur. Then I lick my lips, knowing that the guard will hear my soft taunt as a come-on.

Later my love...

First things first.

My act is working. The guard is too distracted to notice all the toys, which will get my ass, and my asset, off this godforsaken island. In my clutch bag are my ID (a Mexican driver's license that identifies me as "Lucinda Gutiérrez"), a nondescript lipstick, a seemingly innocent compact, a change purse that holds a few coins, and a rosary with a small metal cross.

Here's the plan: Once we're alone in one of the prison's flimsy straw love shacks, I'll clue Hector in on the fact that nookie is out, but a run for the gate is in. Unfortunately, that should keep the smirk on his face. Then I'll slap one of my tiny, but strong, neo-magnetic earrings onto the shack's center pole before shooting the other earring—attached to the zip line hidden in my rosary—out the shack's window with my lipstick case, which is really a miniature missile launcher. The missile's GPS system will lead it to a three-person submarine anchored about thirty feet below high tide and about two hundred feet offshore, where Jack is waiting for us. Once the zip line's magnet has locked onto the exterior antechamber of the sub, we'll roll off this hot hunk of rock using my GPS-driven ribbed bracelet as a pulley.

Since subs are the new vehicle of choice for running drugs between Mexico and the United States, El Chihuahua should feel right at home.

Besides, prison has given him time to get used to tight quarters.

Between the sub's cloaking system and a submersion depth of sixty feet, we will be able to maneuver past any Mexican patrol boats. At a cruising speed of eighty nautical miles per hour, we should surface at the dock of our safe house in the posh tourist enclave Cabo San Lucas in three hours, tops. There, we'll debrief El Chihuahua as to the whereabouts of the Quorum's villa, and get the necessary entry data.

After turning Hector over to his Witness Protection detail, Jack and I will break into the villa, download all files on the master computer's hard drive onto a flash drive and then plant a worm that will allow us to stop Carl from whatever he's got planned in order to impress his new BFFs.

If we accomplish our mission, Acme will learn the identities of the Quorum's new players, and break up the organization once and for all.

My slow stroll through the prison courtyard is serenaded by the jeers and come-ons of the prisoners who, for this month anyway, are unlucky in love. "*Siéntate en mi cara, perra...*" and

"*Quiero que me chupe...*" are the two most common ones shouted so often, and by so many that, to my ear, they sound like a mantra.

I ignore them, and I certainly won't translate them now for you.

I'm too much of a lady for that.

Hector's lawyer has arranged for his client to be assigned the last love shack on the left. I'm sure Hector is in there now, waiting for me. It's perfectly situated for this mission because it is the closest one to the island's north shore, where the submarine is anchored.

I've almost reached the shack when a guard prods my backside with his semi-automatic rifle. "*No no no, puta! Para ahi! El Chihuahua se encuentra en la torre, allí.*"

Ah, hell. Turns out that our little tryst has been moved to another location.

He's pointing to the rickety stairwell that leads to the top of the tower, which, unlike the shack, is made of solid rock. It's too narrow to hold more than one room at the very top, which has only one high, tiny window barred with wrought iron.

As if that matters. If we're in there, the zip line will never reach its final destination: the sub.

"Plan B?" I whisper, just loud enough for Jack to hear me. The wooden staircases are steep, and rickety.

"Dollface, there is no Plan B. Frankly if it was up to me, you'd take a shiv to the slime bucket and waltz out of there. But orders are orders." I hear Jack swiping away on his iPad as he tries to figure another way out for all of us.

Including the odious Hector.

There is just one outdoor landing before the ground floor: on the fourth flight of stairs. I try to keep my head up so that Jack's reconnaissance is easier, but it's difficult because my heels are getting caught on every other step. To hell with that. As I bend down to slip out of them, the guard bringing up my rear murmurs, "*Culo lindo, pero sus piernas son tan flácidas.*"

Should I be flattered he says my ass is cute—or pissed because he thinks my thighs are flabby?

"Hey, what did I tell you? Just twenty minutes on an elliptical would do wonders," Jack says. "No more of that tiny jiggle of cottage cheese on your upper thighs."

In any language, the extension of my middle finger tells both of them what I think of their opinions.

We are in the tower's turret, seven flights up.

"*Llamamos a esta suite la luna de miel,*" the guard says with a snicker.

Yeah, right. Some honeymoon suite.

I'm the first to arrive. I scan the room so that Jack can also see what we've got to work with—

Which ain't much. The room is tiny, and its window, high

above my head, is too small to squeeze through, even if it weren't railed.

There is a double bed on one side, and a dresser on another.

"Jeez! Slim pickings," he mutters. "Okay here's what I figure: first, when the guard leaves, give him a sweet kiss goodnight."

That's code for knocking him out. One of my lip wands, Cherry Noir, should do the trick since it has a top coat of Rohypnol.

"The lock is old and easy to pick," Jack continues. "By the time you do, I'm guessing your physical trainer there will be asleep in the chair outside the door. You can take his semiautomatic. You shouldn't meet anyone else on the stairwell on your way down. From that fourth story landing, you'll have just enough line and gravitational pull to make the jump."

Jack's tell is the small cough he gives after this lie.

Hearing it now, I realize that my chances of getting El Chihuahua out of here will be slim at best.

I finger the rosary, just in case—

Until I slice off the tip of my nail on the zip line. Ay, caramba!

Jack is not done making my day. "By the way, the mirror over the dresser is also a webcam, so give me about two minutes of steady bump and grind. I'll put it on a loop, then hack into the feed with it. The boys won't even realize that the show is a repeat."

Just great. I don't look forward to feeling El Chihuahua's paws all over me, but I'll get over it.

What this girl won't do for her country.

CHAPTER 17

SURVIVING A BAD BLIND DATE

Blind dates can be fun...with the right one!

Sadly, your odds are only 14.7 percent that a blind date will be worth any more than ten minutes of your time. For the other 85.3 percent, you're frantically tugging your earlobe, which is the agreed-upon signal to your gal pal (who sits at an adjacent table, but pretends not to know you) to call your cell phone with some made-up emergency that gets you out of blind date purgatory.

After your great escape, she'll commiserate with you about your dire state of spinsterhood as well as the origin of the term "blind date," over several very dry martinis. Perhaps you need to be blind to survive these meet and greets? Perhaps you were blindsided to accept one?

At this low point, some guy on the other side of the bar hones in on the conversation and buys your next round. He's sort of cute, and conversation with him is scintillating.

It's not until he asks your gal pal if she needs a lift home–and she says yes–that you realize he was the date you just ditched.

It wasn't his looks or his personality that blinded you to him, but your ego.

Then again maybe not, when you consider that old saying, "the difference between a pig and a stallion is three martinis."

El Chihuahua is thin, short, bald, and has bulging eyes.

Now his nickname makes sense.

Above his orange jumpsuit, there isn't an inch of his body that isn't covered with tattoos. Odd words and long lines of numbers run in and around his neck, and over and around his scalp.

Freaky.

Scary.

The way he licks his lips as he looks me up and down, you'd think I was a pork chop.

I try not to shudder as I tantalize him with a long lingering kiss.

While he and the guard exchange smirks, I apply more lip gloss. This time, it's the *Cherry Noir*. Then I slip my hand into the guard's, and walk him to the door. "Adios, amigo," I whisper, before fluttering my lashes and laying on a kiss he won't forget.

When he wakes up, that is.

He stumbles out, too woozy to lock the door behind him.

Great. That gives me one less thing to worry about.

Okay, show time. Smile pretty for the cameras.

My leading man thinks that the simper on my face and the sweet nothings I whisper in his ear are meant for him. In fact, I'm playing to the camera.

In no time at all El Chihuahua has grown by leaps and bounds.

One part of him, anyway.

It takes Hector only a few seconds before he's out of his orange jumpsuit. It's not just his head and his neck that's inked, but every part of his body, like some sort of Sudoku manifesto.

Weird.

The buttons on my blouse are too delicate for his stubby fingers, so he just rips them off. After a few moments of letting him paw at my breasts, I pull him with me onto the floor, below the webcam's lens—

And in a nanosecond I've got the zip line to his neck. I only have to yank it once to get his attention. When he feels my heel on his rotator cuff, his groans are loud and steady.

The boys on the monitor can't see anything, but what they hear sounds like a man in ecstasy. *Perfect.*

After three minutes of this, I hear Jack mutter, "Cut..." Then a moment later. "And print."

The loop is engaged. Show's over. *About damn time...*

I twist Hector's arm behind his back and yank him onto his feet. But before he can scream out in pain, I hiss, "I'm your ride out of here, asshole, so behave yourself, or I'll leave you to *Los Corazónes Rojos*' hit squad. They can't wait to cut out your heart and keep it as a souvenir."

He grins up at me. "Don't like to mix business with pleasure, eh, bitch? What a shame." He eyes me longingly.

He has only the faintest trace of an accent. Heck, the guy graduated cum laude from Wharton School of Business, so that's to be expected. I shake my head in wonder. "Why am I not surprised that you've got a lot of friends in high places? Funny, though, none of them cared enough about you to get you out of this joint."

He shrugs. "Until now. What do you want so badly, that you're willing to do me the favor?"

"You built the Quorum's safe house. You're going to tell me where it is, and give me the floor plan. In return, you'll be freed on U.S. soil and put into Witness Protection."

His smirk is back. He thinks a moment, then taps the side of his head. "No problem. It's all here."

Satisfied, I release my grip.

Big mistake. He grabs my breasts for a quick feel, then crams his tongue down my throat—

And promptly passes out.

My lipstick is El Chihuahua's kiss of sleep.

"Aw, heck," Jack mutters in my ear. "Well now, this ought to be fun. I guess you're going to have to carry him out."

"In heels? And on that staircase? You're kidding, right?"

"I wish I were, babe. It's either that, or hard time for you in Santa Martha Acatitla. We'll get a few conjugal visits, but...well, let's just say it ain't the One & Only Palmilla Resort, if you catch my drift—which, by the way, is where I made your post-mission birthday reservation. Just imagine: our very own villa, with an ocean view *and* an infinity pool. Oh, and get this! The soaking tub in the bathroom has a roof that opens to the stars. Cool, huh? Love those fluffy bathrobes. Hey, what say we get his and hers massages while we're there? Better yet, we'll role-play. I'll be Hans the Austrian masseuse, pleasuring the bored British duchess. Then you can be Inga, the Swedish bombshell... Damn, girl, I'm getting horny just thinking about it. Look, the quicker we blow this joint, the sooner I get to admire you in your new thong bikini."

After what he just said about me having cottage cheese thighs, he'll be lucky to get me out of that fluffy bathrobe.

But then, I remember that naughty smile of Jack's when he teases me, like now.

And the way in which his pale, green eyes darken when he's worried about me. Not to mention how great it will feel when his long, strong arms pull me close to his broad chest.

I can't wait to feel his hungry kisses on the back of my neck, on my lips, my breasts.

Just thinking about what will be waiting for me under Jack's robe gives me all the motivation I need to get the hell out of here.

Not that he needs to know that. "You had me at prison," I murmur instead.

With a sigh, I hoist El Chihuahua over my back and totter out the door.

My hike down the steep, winding stairwell is accompanied by a duet of snores: the guard's, and El Chihuahua's. By the time we reach the fourth story platform, my back is aching. Hector is one hundred and thirty pounds of pure pain.

And let's not forget, he's also naked. *Ewwwwwww*....

I push him up against the stucco wall. He slumps into a corner, but at least he's still standing. Good. As long as he stays out of my way.

"Donna, remember, you're just barely within the line of fire, and you've only got one shot. When you take it, be sure to lean over the edge as far as possible. I'll site you on GPS."

"Gotcha." I fumble to take off my earrings. I loop one through the zip cord. Then I hook the other to the lip-gloss missile launcher, leaning over as far over the banister as I can, toward the side facing the water.

"More to the right," Jack murmurs. "No, you've gone too far. Head left, just a bit... Perfect! Okay, now—"

A bullet whizzes past my nose.

Another one hits the stucco wall behind me.

A third one pierces El Chihuahua in the thigh. He groans loudly and then rouses from his sleep with a long string of Spanish curses.

My instinct is to put down the missile launcher and staunch the spurt of blood. *We can't lose our asset.*

Jack's shout sets me straight. "Donna, do it! *Now!*"

I press the button on the missile launcher. The zip line whistles as it flies out over the rocky beach below.

The guard who has spotted us is shouting now. The other guards are either herding the prisoners out of the yard and back into their cells, or running in our direction.

I lasso the zip line over a heavy wood beam above our heads, then clasp my open compact pulley on the zip line. All the while, El Chihuahua roars out in pain. "You bitch! You got me shot! My lawyer said this was going to be a smooth op—"

To shut him up, I elbow him in the gut. No pain, no gain, right?

As long as all the pain is his.

He doubles over, which makes it easier for me to wrap one end of my belt around my wrist, then the other around one of his, shove him over the side, and leap after him.

A spray of bullets race after us as we hurtle over the palm trees flanking the beach. With just a few seconds to go before we fall into the ocean, I yell, "Hold your breath, asshole!"

His eyes get big as he shouts back! "*Ay, dios mio*! No! I—I can't swim!"

Now he tells me.

We hit the water with the velocity of a cannonball. The sub is just thirty feet below the surface, close enough that we won't get the bends. We would have popped back up if the pulley's GPS system wasn't honed in on the submarine's outer chamber, which is set to close after us, draining water and filling with oxygen before the main cabin opens.

What I haven't counted on is that El Chihuahua would panic. He grabs me around the neck, as if I'm a flotation device. With my free hand, I try to fight him off, but the more I struggle, the tighter he holds onto me.

My lungs feel as if they are about to burst.

A dark shadow circles us slowly. Proof that the Grim Reaper not only walks the Earth, but swims the oceans...

El Chihuahua feels it, too. I can tell because he lurches forward and his eyes pop wider, if that's possible. His mouth widens with a silent scream. He's thrashing frantically. The bubbles around us rise furiously, all pretty and pink—

With El Chihuahua's blood.

Apparently, his injured leg has attracted a shark.

The crunch of bone against the great white's bicuspids roars, like a sonic boom, through the murky water. Jaws and I are playing tug of war with Hector. I fight the urge to let go of him and save myself. The only thing that may save his life—and mine—is the speed in which we're racing toward the sub.

I'm still holding onto him—really, to what is left of him—when

I slam into the submarine's antechamber.

Pissed that his brunch has been rudely interrupted, the shark rams the sub again and again, rocking it from side to side. Gasping for air, I choke as I scream to Jack, "Let's get the hell out of here!"

When the engine kicks in, the sub pitches forward, and I flip over—

Onto what used to be Hector Negrón de la Moraga, which is now just a severed torso and bald head. His bulging eyes stare into mine, accusing me of fucking up royally.

Yep, he's right.

Along with the salt water sieving through the antechamber's drainpipe is the last of El Chihuahua's blood, some of his entrails, and my vomit.

CHAPTER 18

WHAT TO DO WHEN YOU DON'T LIKE HIS FRIENDS

You've met the guys who hang with your new boyfriend, and you're less than impressed. He may be your Han Solo, but his buds could pass for rejects from the Star Wars bar!

On one hand, you feel guilty passing judgment this way. Then again, maybe you have a reason to be concerned. If they're losers, maybe he's one, too. Here are a few telltale signs that he needs a classier set of friends:

1: They greet you by saying, "Hubba, hubba!"

2: When you reach out to shake the hand of one of his bros, you find it up your skirt.

3: Half of these dudes show up with bodyguards.

4: The other half show up with an ATF squad on their tail.

5: They never remember your name. Instead, they call you Chick, Chica, Babe, Doll, or Bitch.

6: Their way of saying "Thank you" is to burp.

Taken collectively, all of these idiosyncrasies indicate that your main squeeze needs a new entourage. Should he (a) balk, (b) bitchslap, or (c) laugh in your face when you suggest that he consider more refined company, take it as a very broad hint that he's not your Mr. Right.

Then take his lowrider, ram it into the nearest ditch, and set it on fire. Doing so will be your subtle hint that you've moved on.

"Well, I guess half an asset is better than none." Count on Jack to look at the bright side.

"Think so? Good. I'll let you explain that to Ryan." My teeth are still chattering. That's to be expected, considering I was just a few seconds away from being a great white shark's dessert course.

I turn my back as I strip out of my wet clothes to the bikini underneath, not because I'm modest in front of Jack (he always admires the view), but because I can't stand to see El Chihuahua glaring at me.

I know why Jack is wincing, and it has nothing to do with the jiggly bits he claims he sees, but because he dreads the thought of calling Ryan. "I guess the sooner we get it over with, the better."

He's right. With or without Hector's intel, we've got to figure out a way to find the Quorum's safe house and break into it.

After setting our GPS coordinates and our speed on autopilot, Jack crouches down for a closer look at El Chihuahua. "There are some strange markings on this dude. Not the usual gangbanger tats. More like... I don't know, calculus or something."

I quit toweling my hair for a closer look. "You're right. But it's certainly a little more complicated than Mary's eighth grade homework." I follow one line of digits, which seem to run on forever but is connected with a plus sign to an equally crazy alphabet.

Could it be . . .?

"Oh my God! Jack, this is some sort of code!" I circle El Chihuahua's torso. "By the look of things, the guy's whole body is a database!"

"If that's the case, then I hope Jaws didn't munch on what we need. Let's show old Hector here to Arnie. He'll know if these are ciphers—and if so, how to decode them." Jack grabs his iPhone off the control board console and then goes in for a tight shot with the camera app, and takes pictures of what's left of Hector. I'm surprised he doesn't pass out, what with the sickening condition of Hector's corpse.

The way Hector's eyes follow me makes me want to gag again.

I try to shake it off, but it's hard to forget his shit-eating smirk as he tapped his head and boasted, "*It's all up here...*"

I grab Jack's arm. "I think I know which one to decipher!

When I asked him about the Quorum's villa, he pointed here." I shiver as I put my finger over Hector's left ear.

"That gives us a place to start." Jack tosses me the iPhone. "But go ahead and take pictures of every inch of your friend. The more samples we supply Arnie, the easier it will be for him to break the cipher. In any event, it's time I call Ryan."

He's given me the easier of the two tasks.

I'll thank him later, in a way I know he'll appreciate.

First, I click off a few shots of the tattoo over Hector's ear. Then I move the iPhone's lens ever so slightly, to another section of Hector's head.

Rest in peace, Hector. You smart ass.

Turns out you were certainly smarter than you looked.

As I snap away, Jack radios into Acme. In no time at all, Ryan's gruff bark is echoing through the submarine. "How's the party?"

"Bad news." Jack pauses. "It got crashed. A shark ate our Chihuahua."

Ryan's curses would make a sailor cringe. When, finally, he calms down, Jack adds, "But we saved enough of him that I think we may still have a chance to save this operation. The guy seems to have written his life story on his bod. You'll see what we mean. We're transmitting now. Have Arnie take a look. Maybe he can make something out of it. Tell him to start with the first code we send, the one over Hector's left ear. Donna thinks he indicated that it's the magic number."

He gives me the high sign. Within a few minutes, I've texted the .jpeg in question, followed by all the other tats, too.

"If you're right, it's the nuttiest thing I've ever heard." Despite the doubt we hear in his voice, the next thing we know, Ryan is shouting to Arnie to get on it.

The line is silent for too long. Finally, Arnie's jubilant shout confirms our suspicions. "Damn, this is awesome! My guess is that the computer will crack it within the hour."

Jack's lips graze my forehead with a congratulatory kiss.

For the first time since I saw that godforsaken island, I'm breathing easy.

But not for long. The submarine's engine lets loose with a bang and a wheeze—

Then silence.

Not good.

Only the emergency lights keep us from groping around in complete darkness.

I'm almost afraid to ask, but someone has to. "What the hell happened?"

Jack checks the life support data on the control console. "Looks like our battery died. We have, at the most, another thirty minutes of back-up power and oxygen."

Unfortunately, we're still one-hundred-twenty-two nautical miles from Cabo.

Jack shakes his head. "We've got to capsize quickly, before

this sardine can sinks like a stone." He tosses the radio receiver and the iPad at me. "Radio Ryan. Tell him to send a helicopter for us. He can track our whereabouts with the iPad, via its GPS coordinates. When you're done, put both in waterproof pouches along with our ops gear, while I inflate the portable DSRV. And as much as I'd personally prefer you in that bikini, I'm guessing you'd be more comfortable if you wore a wetsuit when we get topside."

Thank goodness our sub is equipped with a Deep Submergence Rescue Vehicle.

Suddenly, I remember Hector. "But... what about him?"

Jack laughs and then gives me a swift kiss. "Sweetheart, this isn't *Weekend at Bernie's*. We're not dragging him along. If his tats are encoded, we've gotten what we came for."

He's right. Hector's fate is a burial at sea.

Not mine. Somewhere thirty feet above us is a piña colada with my name on it.

And a date with the Quorum.

After explaining the reality of our situation to Acme, I pack up our op gear and stow it securely inside the DSRV. Then I jump into a wetsuit and fit a scuba mask over my face.

When Jack gives me the high sign, I push the button to the sub's exterior antechamber—

Nothing. Won't open.

I pound on the button, then on the door. Nada. Zip.

I shrug. "Your turn."

Jack grabs a crowbar from the utility closet and tries to pry open the door of the antechamber. Granted, he's six-foot two-inches of gumption, charm, and sinewy muscle, but even he's not Superman, and it ain't budging.

My eyes scan the cabin. The only portion of the hull that is not made of reinforced fiberglass is the glass bubble at the top of the submarine.

I point to it. "The bubble is just big enough for the DSRV to squeeze through it. I say we strap ourselves into it, then we break the glass with the portable ejection system we have in our ops gear. We can also use the ejector to propel the DSRV to the surface. We'll cut loose after we're clear of the sub."

"Works for me." He stares up at it. "Okay, get into position and hold tight. I'll launch on the count of three."

I huddle into the DSRV and wrap my wrists tightly around the straps on the inside of its hull. Jack follows suit. It's not the best of circumstances for cuddling, but hey, it could be worse.

He shouts, "Two...and *three—*" then pulls the trigger on the ejector.

Under water, the usual shriek of shattering glass is dulled to a thud and a *whoosh*. But instead of sprinkling down on us, we fly upward after it.

As we hurtle toward the surface, the tiny shards sparkle like shiny guppies as they float away.

The real fish scurry off in a panic.

I know I should be scared, too. Instead, I'm calm because Jack is holding on to me, as if he'll never let me go.

Of course he won't. Because he loves me.

Like he said: always and forever.

CHAPTER 19

WHEN TO SAY Y-E-S TO S-E-X

So, when is it okay to say yes to sex?

Here are three sure fire signs that you're both ready for the kind of intimacy that leads to the right kind of ring (that is, engagement, as opposed to cock):

Sign Number One: You can't keep your hands off each other. This includes (a) above the waist, (b) below the waist (c) over your clothes, and (d) under your clothes.

Sign Number Two: He whines and begs, "Please? Pretty please? I promise it won't hurt!" He's right, it won't hurt. Unless, afterward, he never calls you again. Should that be the case, feel free to make him hurt as well. Recommended method: a zap from a taser gun.

Sign Number Three: You're over forty. At that point, (a) it's time to give up the ghost that you'll find anyone else who finds you desirable, (b) you deserve to be called something other than "spinster"; and (c) if you don't do it now, your lady bits will dry up like a sun-parched prune rotting on the dusty ground of a Sonoma orchard.

In that case: Just. Do. It.

A fuzzy peach sun is melting into the jade horizon. Hot-pink clouds float around the baby-blue sky, as if in God's lava lamp until, finally, the sun's last rays flicker out, revealing starry pinpricks in the indigo night.

Our three-hour sunbath has browned Jack's face, but it turns pink at my touch.

I touch him often.

I am still holding onto him for dear life.

For the past three hours, our emergency raft has been slapped silly by foamy whitecaps. Although our wetsuits have kept us dry and the wind has finally died down, the night air is chilly enough that we shiver as we lay in each other's arms.

"Acme is sure taking its sweet time getting here," I sigh.

"Maybe the helicopter hit some headwinds coming out of Los Angeles. Fine by me. I'm enjoying a few hours of down time." He closes his eyes, which have darkened to the color of the sea. "Hey, what do you say we make the most of it?"

"Ha! If you think this rubber dinghy is my idea of a romantic getaway, you're mistaken. After sitting in this thing for three hours, I'll need that massage more than ever."

"Your wish is my command. Turn over." Even in the dark, I can make out Jack's playful grin.

"I'd take you up on it, but if this boat goes a'rockin, Señor Shark may come a 'knockin' again, and unfortunately, we've launched our last missile." I toss him the empty ammo cache to make my point.

He laughs. "Okay, I hear you. But I do have something else to keep us busy until the chopper shows up. I was going to save your birthday gifts for after we'd made love in our very own seaside cottage, but I'll let you have them now."

He pulls a small red heart-shaped box from his ops bag, and hands it to me. "For you, milady."

"Really?" I can feel myself blushing. I hesitate only a second before untying the box.

Inside is tiny pink doll, a baseball covered in autographs, a Magic 8-Ball, homemade cookies shaped like hearts and wrapped in cellophane—

And a jeweler's box.

I clear my throat. "*Hmmm*. Interesting combination."

"Go ahead, read the tags. But save the 8-Ball for last."

I would have guessed he'd have asked that of the jeweler's box.

I pick up the baseball. The autographs are from players with the Los Angeles Dodgers, my son's favorite team. Pinned to it is a note:

Dear Mom,

For your birthday, I've cleaned out the garage in order to earn enough money to take you and me to a ballgame—only you'll have to drive us, because even though it's a date, I'm not legal yet.

Your loving and adorable son,

Jeff

"Very thoughtful," I say with a smile. "Especially the part where he points out I should do the driving—considering you've been giving him lessons on the sly."

Jack ducks his head in mock shame. "You know about that, eh?"

I nod. "I overheard him boasting about it to Cheever."

"Every kid in the sticks drives the family truck, or the tractor."

"Lousy excuse, Jack. We live in Hilldale, which is suburbia, not Farmville."

"Hey, you never know. It may come in handy some day. If it's any consolation, he's already a much better driver than Mary."

I punch him in the arm. "Some role model you are! That's all I need, Mary and her twelve-year-old girlfriends rolling the car out of the driveway at night in order to meet their boyfriends for a joyride."

"Like you did, I'm guessing?"

That stops me cold. Yeah, okay. Maybe. Not that I'd ever admit it to her, let alone him.

Time to change the subject and get that smirk off his face. I pick up the cookies. "Yum, what do we have here?"

The attached note says:

Dear Mom,

I made your favorites, chocolate peanut butter! Unfortunately, they're a little burned on the bottom! Usually, I have you yelling at me to watch the timer, and this time I did it as a surprise while you were gone, so I'm sorry! Just don't eat them all at once! I noticed that your thighs jiggle just a bit... but not much!

xoxoxo and happy birthday always,

Mary

Yep, that stops me mid-bite.

Jack is puzzled. "What's wrong?"

"Um... nothing."

Instead, I take the doll in hand. I recognize the haphazard block lettering in the note tied to her wrist as Trisha's handiwork:

DEAR MOMMY, HAPPY BIRTHDAY! I HOPE YOU AND DADDY MAKE LOTS OF SANDCASTLES AT THE BEACH. MY DOLL WILL HELP. SHE WILL ALSO KEEP YOU FROM MISSING ME. LOVE, TRISHA

I tear up. "This is the first birthday I've been away from them."

"Don't forget, you left them with some pretty fancy going away presents. Those chocolate bars you made from scratch in the shape of their names were awesome." Very gently, Jack swipes at the tear that is rolling down my cheek, but he can't wipe away the heaviness I feel in my heart at the thought that maybe, just maybe, one day I may not come back to her.

If that were to happen, she too would get a note from me, telling her why:

Because I kill bad guys.

Jack knows how to change the subject. He hands me the ring box.

It is the moment of reckoning...

Wrong.

Yes, it is a very important piece of jewelry, but not, as I presumed, an engagement ring.

It is the antique locket necklace I had inherited from my mother.

"You always wear it at home, but you didn't take it on this op,"

Jack says.

"Should something ever happen to me... well, let me put it this way, I would never want anything to happen to this locket, too. It was my mother's. I know it will be important to the children one day."

How can I explain to him that inside is the only picture of Carl left in existence?

The rest of them disappeared when he did: the night Trisha was born.

Should I fail at my lifelong mission—to defeat the Quorum—I'd want my children to learn about their real father. Between this locket and the handbook I've left for them in my curio cabinct, they will finally know the truth.

I pray to God that day never comes.

Not that I can say any of this to Jack. Instead, I lift my hair off my neck. "But hey, it's brought us luck thus far. Will you do me the honor?"

After clasping it, he kisses me there.

The warm memory of his lips still lingers on the nape of my neck as he hands me the Magic 8-Ball. "Okay now it's time for my gift. You get to shake it three times. Whatever pops up is something that will take place when all of this is behind us."

Wishful thinking.

But seriously, will the Quorum ever go away?

I have to believe it will. And it better be tonight.

In any event, it's a wonderful dream to share.

I give him the smile we both need right now. "Sounds like fun." I shake it hard, six times. "Okay, here's the first answer: 'Without a doubt.'"

He laughs. "That fits a lot of questions."

"You're right. I've got one, but first promise not to laugh, okay?" I take a deep breath. "Jack, seriously, should we be worried that the Cavalry hasn't shown up? Granted, we've got another seven hours of battery time in the iPad."

"I know you're still spooked by the shark, Donna, but admit it. We've both been through worse."

He's right. To let him know that I've shaken off my fears, I take the ball and twist it right, then left, before taking a peek. "Okay, now it says 'Don't count on it.'"

His smile disappears. "Care to take another guess?"

I'm almost afraid to voice my fear. "I'm hoping the question is, 'Will you ever leave me?'"

I don't need to add, *Like Carl did?*

I have my answer in the way his eyes look deep into mine.

As if there is nothing in life more important to him.

Did Carl ever love me like this? Maybe. But it was a long time ago.

But Carl is gone.

And Jack is here to stay.

I know this because the Magic 8-Ball deems it so.

Smiling, I shake the ball one last time: "It says 'Signs point to yes.'"

"Good. Because the question is 'will you marry me?'"

His mouth hovers over mine, longingly. Finally our lips meet in a gentle kiss.

If floating on a raft in the Pacific after seeing a man eaten by a shark teaches you anything, it's that life is too short and too uncertain to waste on coy flirtations. Jack's tongue knows the inside of my mouth as well as his own. It also knows the curve of my shoulder, where it lingers oh so longingly.

Very slowly, he unzips my wetsuit, releasing my breasts. His lips tickle me as they roam over them. As much as he enjoys their plump softness, his prime objective is my nipples, which the cool air (or is it his tongue?) has enlarged, making them so, so stiff—

Just like Jack.

His wetsuit can't hide the fact that his cock is now long and hard.

I am aching to have him inside me.

My fingers can't unzip his wetsuit fast enough. He must feel the same way about mine because he strips off mine, too—first the left arm, then the right one—until it hangs low around my hips. With one yank he pulls it down around my ankles, but holds me steady so that I don't tumble out of the raft.

After that little project, my string bikini is a piece of cake. He unties one side, then the other. He holds it up and a breeze catches it and lifts it up and over the waves.

Jack isn't watching because he's too busy admiring the view between my legs. A long index finger and thick thumb are working in tandem at making me throb for him.

"Jack, I don't think . . ." is all I can gasp.

I want to explain to him why I can't say yes to his proposal.

Not yet, anyway.

Not until Carl is out of our lives, forever.

Jack enters me with a deep thrust. In no time at all we find our rhythm, along with that sweet spot deep within me. The combination of joy and ecstasy has me throwing back my head so that I am looking skyward—

Just in time to see a shooting star race across the galaxy.

By the time it disappears somewhere far beyond Orion, the moans from our passion-fueled orgasms have scared the fish away.

The helicopter hovering overhead is a different story.

Ryan's voice shouts down at us through a bullhorn, "So, tell me, was it as good for you as it was for me?"

CHAPTER 20

WILL HE JUMP THROUGH HOOPS FOR YOU?

There are three true measures of any man's commitment to a relationship. Here they are, in reverse order of importance:

Measure #3: He's keen on washing your hair, and giving you mani-pedis. Don't laugh! A man who will do this for his sweetheart is a man worth waiting for. (Hopefully his heartache over the breakup with his boyfriend won't last forever.)

Measure #2: He remembers all major dates in your lives together: your birthday, the anniversary of the day you met, the anniversary of the day you moved in together, the anniversary of the day you first whipped him into a frenzy. (Or just whipped him. And couldn't stop. And claimed you forgot his safety word.)

Measure #1: He doesn't balk when you ask him to commit murder to avenge your honor. Granted, your command that he do so shouldn't be given lightly! That said, your waste-not, want-

not list should include frenemies, old boyfriends, or anyone who jumps ahead of you in line. Why? Because if he's stupid enough to kill for you, he's stupid enough to leave a trail to your doorstep.

(In fact, if you ask him to make this sacrifice, it's time for a new boyfriend to exterminate the old one. At that point, you can delete "old boyfriends" from your waste-not, want-not list.)

"Genius! The guy was sheer genius!" Arnie's shrieks are just as annoying as the helicopter's thumping blades. "Did you know Hector owns a bank, too? In a country like this, I guess it's the safest way to hide anything."

"You mean the location and the floor plan for the Quorum's villa is in some bank's safety deposit box?" I yell back.

"In fact, Hector has a whole vault reserved for his company, *Ay Chihuahua Construction, at Banco Regional de California Sur*." Ryan keeps a steady gaze on the villas dotting the hills surrounding Cabo San Lucas. I guess he's too embarrassed to look me in the eye. Hell, he's already seen too much of me. "This big hoedown Carl has planned tonight will be easier for both of you to get lost in a crowd. From what Valentina's intel shows, it's the Who's Who we've been waiting for: not the foot soldiers, but the Quorum's new investors. Everyone there is a suspect, so you'll both be wearing digital camera lenses in order to take lots of pictures."

I shake my head in disbelief. "Isn't hanging together for a

meet-and-greet a risky proposition?"

"Don't fool yourself. These guys are up to something. It's all about the mission." Finally, Ryan looks me in the eye. "But they're not above mixing business with pleasure. Every socialite and celebrity in town for the holiday has been sent an invitation, making it harder for the Quorum's leaders to be spotted. But first things first: that little withdrawal." Ryan turns to me. "Donna, you'll divert the two bank guards and then hit them with Roofie pricks, so they'll doze off for an hour or so. As a safeguard, Arnie will set up a loop on the bank's security cameras. Jack, when Donna gives you the high sign, you'll break into the vault and pull the drawer with the villa's floor plans."

Jack nods. "So you think this op should take a half-hour, tops."

"That's the plan. Let's hustle. We've got a party to crash."

The chain-smoking security guard on his break thinks it's his lucky night when he comes to the rescue of a *chica bonita* with a tight, short skirt and no matches to light her own cigarette.

As he cups his hand around his lighter's flame, my thank-you is a jab to his neck with a tiny needle injected with Rohypnol.

His eyes cross as he stumbles into my arms. Cradling him, I tap loudly on the glass door to get the attention of the second guard and shout at the top of my lungs, "*Oye, tú! El señor guardia! Tu amigo necesita ayuda! Él pudo haber tenido un ataque al corazón!"*

He's out of his chair in a flash. My assessment—that his partner had a heart attack—has him in a panic. When he leans beside me to help me unbutton the fallen guard's shirt, he also gets pricked with a Roofie injection.

"We're in," I murmur just loud enough to be picked up by the ops team's audio receivers.

A moment later, Jack, dressed as a security guard, turns the corner. He grabs one of the sleeping beauties and I lug the other over to the security desk.

Jack nods at me. "When they wake up, you'll be just a fond memory."

"Go down that corridor on the right," Arnie's voice mutters in our ear. "The vault is the third one on the left. You're looking for Box Number 1761, by the way."

When we get to the designated vault, we scan its lock with a digital sensor reader, and in a jiffy the entry code reveals itself. Before opening the vault, we pull on our infrared goggles. The security sensors look like a red spider's web that stretches from one side of the room to another.

Jack gives a long, low whistle. "Arnie, I'll scan the room top to bottom, starting on the left. Donna will do the same, from the right. Holler if you see the box."

Starting at the right side of the room, I follow Jack's lead, glancing from top to bottom of each row. Finally, Arnie says, "Jack, stop! Fourth row on the left, about three boxes from the top. Which one of you is best at Limbo? It's going to take a contortionist to get over there, let alone to pull it out of the wall without setting off the alarm."

Jack shrugs. "Is there any way you can turn off the sensors?"

"Ha! I wish . . . No, wait! I can raise the heat on the vault's thermostat, to 99 degrees. That will offset any readings it takes from your body heat. But you'll have exactly a minute before it trips an alarm to the bank's central security division."

Jack murmurs, "I'm ready when you are."

There is a moment of silence before we hear Arnie again. "Okay, it's now up around 72 degrees...78...81...85...89...92..."

Yes, we can feel it. In no time, sweat is rolling down our faces.

"It just hit 99 degrees. So make your move," Arnie says.

In a flash, Jack is at the far wall. He pulls Box Number 1761, sets it on the large table in the middle of the room, and goes at it with a carbide pick.

"Hurry, dude! I've got to start lowering the thermostat...like...now." Whenever he's anxious, Arnie's voice goes up an octave. Let's just say he could join any touring company of *Jersey Boys* right about now.

Near the ceiling, faint trails of the infrared sensors are beginning to reappear.

"Yes!" Jack holds up a memory stick for a second, before pocketing it. "Let's go!"

The rays are now crisscrossing the top half of the vault. Jack crouches low as he bounds out of the room, but then he freezes when a red line pierces the floor in front of him.

Another cuts horizontally, waist high.

A third zips right past his head, missing his left ear by a mere inch.

The only thing he can do now is drop onto his belly, and crawl toward the door.

“Move a little to your right,” I direct him. “Good! Okay slowly... slowly... Now roll left, about four feet... Stop! Okay you’re a straight shot to the door.”

He’s got just another five feet to go when three rays angle themselves into a star, directly in his path.

“Jack, freeze! Let me think this through.” I crouch down for a better view. “Can you tuck and roll into a power jump? That would get you through it.”

“What? Are you nuts? Need I remind you that not all of us were cheerleaders in high school?”

“Don’t knock it! It’s the most athletic pursuit, female or male, that schools can offer students. Not to mention it encourages school spirit—Agh! Don’t get me started.” I take a deep breath. “Okay, here’s how we’re going to do it: you’re going to get into a crouch with your arms straight out. I’ll grab your forearms and pull you through, but very slowly, and only about halfway. Once your torso is through the doorway, you’ll have to leap straight out at me or you’ll trip that last ray. Got it?”

He nods with a frown.

I'm sure he'll look at cheerleaders differently, from now on.

If I let him look at them at all.

As he positions himself, I squat down too, directly across from him. "Remember, stay low!"

"Donna, just do it. Before I pull a hamstring or something else," he mutters.

I take his forearms. Slowly I pull him through: arms, head, and torso—

He perches like a heron, balancing himself on one leg as he waits for my final signal—

That I've got his back, or in this case his arms above his elbows.

That he's in the clear.

That I won't let go.

Not on your life.

Certainly not on his.

"Now!" I shout.

He springs toward me.

At the same time, I yank him so hard that he falls on top of me. No bells or whistles, just the sound of our heavy breathing.

His heart is beating as fast as mine. No doubt the jubilant look on his face mirrors my own.

We could high-five, but we kiss instead.

"Yee-*hah!*" Arnie shouts in our ears. "Guys, you did it! ...

Guys? … Anyone there? Either your eyes are closed, or you've gone dark on me… But I can hear you breathing, so… Hey! *The Quorum!* Remember?"

Jack sighs as he rolls off me.

It's party time.

CHAPTER 21

WEDDING BELL BLUES

Let's face it, not every man is marriage material. If you've still got doubts about your Mr. Maybe, here are five surefire clues that he has no intention of walking down that aisle with you:

Clue #1: Every time he catches you writing his surname with the prefix "Mrs." in front of it, he retches all over your new carpet.

Clue #2: You cry at weddings, especially when you find him in the coat closet, feeling up one of the bridesmaids.

Clue #3: When you leap to catch the bride's wedding bouquet, he tackles you to the ground.

Clue #4: You remind him that your biological clock is ticking. He reminds you that he's waiting for Megan Fox to drop Brian Austin Green.

Clue #5: When you show him the wedding dress you've already bought for the big day, he runs out the door, like a mad man. Even the GPS tracker you embedded in him is of no use, since he gnawed off his arm in order to lose it, and you.

Look on the bright side: they don't make one-armed grooms for wedding cake toppers, so he wasn't the right guy for you anyway.

The new Quorum hides in plain sight.

From the cabin of our Stingray 225-SX speedboat, we have a clear shot of its ten-acre hilltop estate, which crowns Sunset Point, high over the sandy beaches cradling Bahia San Lucas.

The forty-two room, three-story villa has a dead-on view of Land's End, where the gentle azure waves flowing south from the Sea of Cortez are slammed into a high flying spray by the roiling jade Pacific. There, you'll find *El Arco*, or "the Arch," a natural stone keyhole carved out of the seaside cliff by wind and surf and God's good graces for the rest of us to gasp in awe at nature's beauty.

The Quorum's event is a black-and-white ball. The invitation in my hand, secured earlier by Ryan, belongs to a dowager heiress too ill to attend, thanks to a few eye drops of Binaca slipped into her chocolate mousse during lunch with her golf partners at the Dunes Course at Diamante. Jack's golden ticket was stolen from the hotel inbox of a producer. (Broadway, not film, so no one should miss him, anyway.)

Not that anyone could be recognized at this shindig in the first place, since everyone will be wearing masks.

"Ah, hell," roars Ryan, when he reads that in the invitation. "There goes the whole purpose of taking pictures."

"Not necessarily," Arnie pipes up. "Depends on the mask. If any parts of their ugly mugs are exposed, our facial recognition software may still pick up enough distinctive features to ID some of the fat cats."

All heads turn to the computer monitor in front of us, where the Quorum's floor plan is displayed.

"Donna, there is a secure elevator hidden in the library, here." Ryan taps a windowless room, accessed through a hallway next to the grand ballroom. "You'll find it behind a bookcase."

"The books look real, but they are all just one big façade—except for *Ulysses*, smack dab in the middle of the third shelf." Arnie explains. "Just tilt it down. I guess they figured no one would ever open that one—and voilà, you're in."

"The elevator goes straight up through the villa, to the top floor," Ryan says. He taps the screen. "It drops you in the only room up there. Once you're inside, go to the console holding the computer."

"You'll insert this thumb drive," Arnie interjects. He's holding up a tiny clear plastic USB flash drive. "It's been programmed to duplicate the computer's data and email files. That should take exactly six minutes. A minute later it will drop a worm into the computer's hard drive, which will then transmit any new data files created or viewed, whether they're loaded onto the Quorum's secure server, or sent to a cloud."

"The sooner, the better," Ryan mutters. "Our cousins have picked up some unsettling chatter on their side of the pond. The surprise attack Carl has planned is taking place at eleven o'clock tonight Pacific Time."

"I guess their little shindig gives every Quorum suspect an alibi, since that's exactly when the party's over-the-bay fireworks show begins."

I'm almost afraid to ask, but I have to do it. "Where will the bomb go off?"

"That's the problem. It's not just one city on the hit list, but fourteen," Ryan answers. "London, New York, Paris, Tokyo, Leningrad, Moscow, Jerusalem, Berlin, Rome, Geneva, Toronto, Argentina, Beijing, and—I'm sorry to say, folks: our hometown, too."

Los Angeles.

My children are in danger.

And I'm not home to protect them.

I want to cry.

No. I want to stop the Quorum.

My floor-length, silver sequined jersey gown is strapless, has a big bow in back, and fits me like a second skin. It looks great with my sleek, chin-grazing platinum-blond wig.

If I find myself in trouble, my ring has a Roofie prick, and my heels truly are stilettos.

Not to mention that I've got a two-inch-long Swiss MiniGun tucked in my bustier. It fires bullets at a speed of 399 feet per second.

Don't worry. The safety is on.

In case the Quorum's security also has face recognition software, my papier-mâché mask makes me a dead ringer for Marilyn Monroe. The crowd is thick enough that both Jack and I have blended in easily. So that I can spot him in this throng of white tuxedos jackets, he wears a traditional Venetian death mask. It is white, almost square, and cut high above the jaw. It covers most of his face with pronounced cheeks, strong flaring nostrils, and just the barest indentation of eyebrows over the eye holes.

My mask is a classic colombina, covering just the top part of my face—nose, eyes, and forehead—before pluming out into a silver headdress.

Our orders are very clear. As Jack circles the crowd so that Arnie can download as many digital impressions as possible, I'll plant the bug, sound the all-clear, and meet Jack at the Stingray, which Arnie has tied up in an inlet behind this pile of stone and stucco.

Whenever a member of the plain-tux goon squad looks my way, I chat up some muckety-muck until I'm in the all-clear. I've recognized a few British soccer players and American basketball players, a handful of Oscar film stars, and way too many Kardashians.

A group of three women break off to find a powder room, and I make it a point to join them. Complimenting one of them on her dress puts me in the thick of their entourage, but I break away when I'm next to the staircase that coils on the wall over the library.

Arnie is right. The wall of books looks real enough, but only one actually moves: Ulysses.

The bookcase slides apart silently. Inside the elevator, there is only one button to push.

Going up—

To take them down.

The ride is slow and silent. Finally, the door opens. A few moments pass for my eyes to adjust to the only light in the room: the glow of the stars reflected in the bay, below the balcony's glass doors. When I do, I see the console. It holds just one thing: a desktop computer.

I pull the memory stick from a tiny waterproof pocket sewn into one of my opera gloves, and input it into one of the computer's USB ports. Immediately the stick does its thing, blinking blue to indicate it is reading files, and loading them into its memory.

I count down the seconds on the computer's digital clock. As if that will make time go any faster.

Finally, the stick flashes green, indicating that the Trojan Horse is being downloaded into the computer's stable of files.

I've just pulled the memory stick from the computer and slipped it back into the tiny waterproof pocket in my glove when a voice behind me says, "I thought I'd find you here."

I look up to find myself staring at Jack's death mask.

He steps out of the shadows. Those broad shoulders are a sight for sore eyes.

"Perfect timing," I scold him. "Let's get out of here."

"What's the rush? Don't you want to stay for the fireworks?"

Aw hell. His voice isn't Jack's.

But yes, I know it...

He is Carl.

"Thanks, but I've already got a date," I purr, as I move closer. "However, since we're together again, there is one thing I'd like to do."

Playfully I run my fingers up the lapel of his tux until I'm close enough to pat his bowtie—

Which I grab with both hands. As I choke him, I murmur, "I want to finish you off once and for all, *you son of a bitch.*"

He wrenches my hands from his neck, then twists my arms behind my back until they ache in agony. I know he'd like to hear me scream from the pain, but I won't give him the satisfaction.

"How did you know I was here?" I ask.

He grins down at me. ""You're one of the most beautiful

women here tonight. Of course I'd want to meet you. And then I saw that necklace. I'd know it anywhere."

Ah, hell. I'd forgotten to take it off when I dressed for the party.

I shrug. "What can I say? It's my favorite."

He yanks off his mask. I gasp when I see his face. It's been altered since the last time we met. His nose is straighter, his eyes are larger, and his cheekbones are more pronounced.

Shave his head and he could pose as the skeleton on a bottle of poison. Why am I not surprised?

Carl laughs at my shock and dismay.

"Don't worry. I'm still the same old Carl you know and love." His hand lingers on my cheek, which he strokes gently. "You still love me, don't you, Donna?"

I spit at him.

He wipes his face with the back of his hand. Then he slaps me.

I don't even flinch, although it smarts like hell.

Instead, I smile. "Frankly, I'm surprised to see you here. I thought learning you'd killed the mother of your child would have left you too bereft to make the rest of us so miserable."

He pulls me closer. "No such luck. As it turns out, as I suspected the Romanian whore's child wasn't mine after all."

"Liar. You're just trying to assuage your guilt."

"Hey, don't take my word for it. Acme did the autopsy. Ask Ryan if you can see the DNA report on the fetus."

"Seriously, Carl, enough with these childish attempts to come between Jack and me! I'd never do that. I don't have to, because I'll always take his word over yours."

"That's easy to do, now that the competition is dead and buried." He shakes his head. "It was a beautiful ceremony, wasn't it? Just the two of you. Oh yeah, and the gimp came late to the party. C'est la vie! Although I do love Paris this time of year. It would be perfect for a second honeymoon. We can leave tonight! Admit it, you've missed me."

I want to spit in his face again. Instead, I smile up at him. I can only imagine how much he hates my smile.

I test that theory by whispering, "Maybe you should refresh my memory as to why that might be the case."

Guess I'm wrong. His lips graze mine gently, then hungrily.

No, I don't resist him. I can't.

Otherwise, my family is doomed.

It is true that hate is a desire just as strong as love. Whereas the latter is now driving an involuntary instinct to enjoy what I am feeling, the former gives me the strength to reach down, gently and slowly—

And pull a stiletto from my right heel.

"Oh yeah," I murmur gently in his ear, "Now I remember."

Then, with a flick of a nail, the knife is open and I stab him again, in his old wound. "I remember I shot you *here*."

He roars in pain. On reflex, he smacks me hard across the

face, and I fall to the floor. By the time I get up again, he has yanked the stiletto from his shoulder. A corsage of blood seems to be growing on his crisp, white tuxedo jacket.

He pulls off my wig and jerks me back up to my feet by my hair. I'm still woozy, and I know he's got to be, too. Still, he's strong enough to drag me through the open balcony doors.

"The fireworks are going off any moment now. I wouldn't want you to miss them."

He's right. Already the party guests are gathered by the pool, counting down the seconds:

...47...46...45...

"You see, my darling wife, thanks to the intel provided by the dearly departed Chinese general Huang Zitong—some of the missiles we'll shoot off tonight are going further than the bay out there. All the way to China, in fact. As well as Russia, England, France, New York. And yes, as close as Los Angeles."

He's holding the knife at my throat, ready to cut my jugular if I scream out.

Despite this, I whisper, "But Mary is there! And Jeff, and Trisha—"

"The children? Believe me, I thought about them. You know, Donna, considering your superb cooking skills, I'd think you'd be the first person to adhere to that old adage, 'If you can't stand the heat, get out of the kitchen.' Time to retire, don't you think? If not for your own sake, then for the kids. That is, if they're still alive after tonight." He shakes his head in mock horror. "You've raised them with absolutely no survival skills! What kind of mother does that make you? If they survive, I'll certainly push even harder for joint custody."

The crowd's singsong shouts are making me dizzy. *22…21…20…*

Doesn't he have a conscience? "Millions of people will die—and for what?"

11…10…9…8…

He smiles down at me. "What do you think? *For money.* Believe me, those in power knew the cost. And guess what? *They refused to pay the ransom.*" That smile of his, which I'll never forget as long as I live, is dazzling, brilliant. "Donna, you and I both know better than anyone—hell, even Valentina knew it! You always pay a price."

"Three! Two! *ONE!*" shouts the crowd.

Then—

Nothing.

Not a thing.

I look at him and shrug. "Oopsy. My bad."

Trisha taught me that one. Rarely does it get her out of trouble.

I don't think it will help me here, either.

At first, he doesn't get it. When he does, he drags me over to the computer, but it's too late. Arnie's bug—in this case, a centipede—dashes around the screen before morphing into a one-finger salute.

"Why, you little bitch! You did it again!"

"Yeah. You see, we housewives have another saying: 'Fuck off.'"

"*Touché*. Well, at least you'll die for a great cause. I'll say so, at your funeral. I'm sure the kids will appreciate it."

This time when he pulls me in close, it's only to rip the locket from my neck. "I'll take this, as a keepsake. Oh yeah, and for old time's sake—"

His tongue is down my throat.

This time I play hard to get. I chomp down hard, and he screams in pain.

He grabs me and drags me to the balcony railing. Over I go—

But my hand catches hold of it, and I'm left dangling. Carl stands over me, his foot poised to crush my hand beneath it. I groan in agony at the pressure he puts on one finger, then another.

All of a sudden, he's groaning, too, from a punch in the kidney—

From Jack.

Jack pulls me back onto my feet while Carl is doubled over—

But Carl doesn't stay that way for very long. Angrily, he rises and kicks Jack in the gut.

Even as Jack stumbles, he takes a swing at Carl, but misses.

The next thing I know, it's Jack who is being choked. As he

hangs half over the balcony, all I can think about is that I'm about to lose the man I love.

No way. Ain't happening.

Once was enough.

Any woman will tell you that there are very few things a mere two inches long that pack a wallop. My Swiss MiniGun is one of them. The bullets may be tiny, but the velocity from just one shot to his right bicep is enough to jerk him away from Jack.

And off balance.

His arms flail like pinwheels in a mad breeze as he tries to straighten up. He almost makes it, too.

But then I snatch my necklace out of his hand.

Oh yeah, and I tip him over the edge with a finger to his bloody wound.

Oopsy. My bad.

Just before he tumbles over the balcony, he looks up at me.

The hatred I see in his eyes will stay with me, always.

No mistaking it for love, that's for sure.

Jack holds me as we stare into the inky abyss below. All we can hear is the crashing surf.

Finally, he kisses me gently on the forehead. "Hey, have you had a chance to think about my proposal?"

I take a deep breath. "My answer is yes—now that I'm free."

"Free? You mean... Wait! *That was Carl?*"

I nod through my tears. “He’s had facial reconstruction. He enjoyed the fact that I didn’t recognize him, but I’ll always know his voice.”

“Damn! Wish I had, since I never got to say two words to him. Those two words being, ‘Fuck you.’”

I can’t help but laugh at that. “You had your hands full, remember? And considering that you’ve been sleeping in his old bed, trust me, I’m sure he had a few choice words for you, too.”

“I’ll just bet he had.”

Had. It all seems so final.

Carl, the father of my children, is dead. And I killed him.

In all fairness, he tried to kill me, too. Four times, in fact. Oh yeah, and obliterate the rest of the world while he was at it.

Seriously, what did I ever see in that guy?

The ruckus behind us—shouts and guns blazing—gives us fair warning that the party is over. For us, anyway.

Jack and I look down. Then we look at each other.

Holding hands, we leap out together—

And pray that the tide below us is deep enough to keep us alive.

As we plummet below the water’s surface, I say prayers that Jack and I live to see another day. That we will get home safely to Mary and Jeff and Trisha.

That for once and for all we’ve proven our love and commitment to each other.

Trust is the rarest of treasures for spies like us.

Finally my fall stops. I open my eyes. For just a few seconds, I am suspended in an underwater prism of immense beauty and wonder. A swarm of tiny rainbow fish darts away, whereas a sea turtle, almost my height, hovers just within reach. I imagine he wonders about the strange creature before him.

Good question.

Mother. Lover. Assassin. Member of the neighborhood welcoming committee.

And soon-to-be divorcee.

Then it hits me: if we survived the fall, maybe Carl did, too.

Oh....

Hell.

But I guess the fact that he's a terrorist gives me strong grounds for divorce.

I feel an arm around my waist. It is clad in a tux jacket. As it hauls me up toward the surface, its shirt cuff glistens, blinding me when it hits a wavering shaft of light.

I can't tell if it belongs to Carl, or to Jack.

A shiver goes up my spine. A torrent of tiny bubbles obscures the view of my savior. As they bombard me, instinctively my eyes shut tight.

All I can do is pray that I'm in the arms of the right man.

We break the surface. His kiss lets me know that it's okay to open my eyes.

Even before I do, I know I have the answer to my prayers.

Jack smiles as he treads water beside me. “I could use that couples’ massage. How about you?” he asks.

“Sounds yummy. Let’s do it,” I answer.

Why not? It’s still my birthday.

Other Novels by Josie Brown

The True Hollywood Lies Series

Hollywood Hunk

Hollywood Whore

Hollywood Heiress
Release Date: 2016

The Totlandia Series

The Onesies - Book 1 (Fall)

The Onesies - Book 2 (Winter)

The Onesies - Book 3 (Spring)

The Onesies - Book 4 (Summer)

The Twosies - Book 5 (Fall)
Release Date: Fall 2015

More Josie Brown Novels

The Candidate

Secret Lives of Husbands and Wives

The Baby Planner